Psychopaths Love

Kiana Mason

Contents

Ferenc Nadasy

It was the night at Nagyecsed, Hungary, and small villages were afar. It was also a tourist site as well because of the Ecsed castle. Ecsed castle was now a ruin, but it was still a tourist attraction for many visitors worldwide. No tourists were allowed to enter the castle except those who worked to clean and preserve it and another man.

The one-man was walking within the castle ruins and into the most preserved part of the castle. The castle was his as he bought it from the government for a decent amount, and he promised that tourists would be allowed to tour it to bring the country more tourism.

However, the man was to decide if the castle would be open, and it was one of those days that it was not. The Ecsed castle once belonged to none other than the infamous blood countess, Elizabeth Bathory. The countess was known to murder young peasant women and use their blood for bathing, for she believed that their blood would preserve her youth. After the countess's death, all else was forgotten, and her children took over the castle and other properties of the Bathory family, but not many knew of her descendants. There were a few, but they were now among the ordinary people, except one.

His name is Ferenc Nadasy, named after Elizabeth Bathory's husband. Ferenc stood at five feet and eight inches tall. He had light olive skin, a muscular build, and a broad face. His black hair was slicked back, and his eyes were black as night and filled with mystery. He kept his beard clean, cut, and nicely shaved. He is one of the many descendants left from his father's side. However, he and his family kept it secret since they didn't want too much attention, especially since they were in high society. His ancestors tried their very best to keep their status. Some failed, while others succeeded. However, his family knew that titles alone would send their children to school to better their status, and Ferenc was part of the success story.

He was known throughout Hungary and Europe and was wanted by many women, and many were after him. On the outside, he was known as handsome, charming, intelligent, and rich, but he wanted the world to know that.

There was another truth to him.

He was sadistic and had no care in the world for the suffering of others. He used others to get to where he was and enjoyed their suffering. Ferenc also had the enjoyment of abusing and torturing women. He would sleep with them and dump them on the street as he viewed them as trash.

Ferenc walked inside the castle and looked at the paintings and belongings that once belonged to his ancestor. He smirked as he remembered the cries and begging from women who wanted him, who wanted his love, affection, and attention. Ferenc would laugh at them, embarrass them. He would hire men to take pictures and videos and post them online, only adding to their humiliation. The middle-aged man would make them seem that they were the insane ones, even if the women tried to explain that he was the insane one.

There were times when some women tried to get revenge, and that was when Ferenc used that to sedate one of his urges.

His urges to...kill. Once, he took a confident woman out on a date, and as she offered to open her legs for him, he took her to one of the castles he owned, and that was when he acted on his urges. He tortured the woman slowly. It made him feel excited and powerful. Ferenc did the deed and killed her; however, he hired his men to make it look like a car accident.

His men dared not to say anything since he knew everything about them and could make their lives hell. Either way, no one would believe them.

Ferenc stopped before the portrait of his ancestor, Elizabeth, and looked at her eyes. He knew that he inherited his blood lust from her.

Victim #1

I t was another week of the same thing. Ferenc had interviews with magazines about his success and business meetings about his companies' well-being. Every single day was nothing but a bore, and there was nothing that brought him excitement.

However, there was one thing.

His urges were getting the best of him, making his body tremble, but it didn't trouble him. Ferenc didn't understand why people like him would try to hold it back; he smirked. Whenever he gave in to his urges, it brought him to life.

The want and need to kill; the blood.

The action alone brought him ecstasy. He looked at his phone and looked at a site; he found a victim. Ferenc was part of a sugar daddy site, and all he had to do was get the most believable but fake profile pictures of a handsome man and create a fake occupation; he got many likes and messages from many women.

It was too perfect.

Ferenc believed that women were pathetic and insolent that wanted men to care for their every need. He just finished talking to a young woman who was nineteen years of age. She hit him up a month ago, and they've been in contact. She had doubts that s such a good-looking man would exist, and she wanted to call. He used a speaking device to hide his voice; it made her believe him.

It was too easy.

He gained her trust, and she told me what she sought. The young woman had no job or interest in working or attending school. She just wanted to live in wealth without doing anything; she was asked about her family life. Her father was never in the picture, and her mother was hardly home since she would travel for work.

It was perfect for him.

They would meet at one of the many homes Ferenc owned in a small village. In actuality, the village was empty. It was bought for tourism to earn a profit. Now, Ferenc was waiting in the house. All the houses were lit to make it seem like people were in the village. He checked the time, and it was almost 9 pm; she would arrive anytime.

The young woman eventually arrived, and excitement filled him. There was a knock on the door, and he opened it. She was a bit chunky than her profile picture but had a pretty face because of the makeup. She had long blonde hair, many freckles on her face, and a bit on her shoulders. She wore a mini black dress that made her breast plumper. Her legs were long and slightly plump; her buttocks were almost seen.

"Typical whore," he thought.

When she saw Ferenc, her eyes widened. "Y-You! It can't be you! You're Ferenc Nadasy!"

"The one and only. Apologies for the profile. I don't want the media to know what I'm doing. I hope you don't mind."

She let out a squeal. "I can't believe it! THE Ferenc Nadasy! I must be dreaming!"

He smirked and motioned her to enter the house. "Please come in. I would love to explain everything to you." Once the young woman entered, Ferenc closed the door and locked it shut. He led her to the dining room, where the food was ready.

They sat on their seats, and Ferenc served the wine; he smiled at her. "I am sure you are wondering why I would be on a sugar baby site. I miss the companionship, but I'm not interested in anything serious."

"Oh, you say that, baby. With me here, who knows, you might change your mind." She took a sip of the wine.

"You seem quite confident in yourself. I like that, Miss..."

"Elina, baby. Trust me when I tell you, I'll treat you right, and you might change your mind."

He raised an eyebrow as he ate a piece of his meat; he also felt annoyed as he looked at Elina. "Eat more and drink your fill; I wouldn't want you to go hungry."

"Don't worry; I won't tell a soul! I wouldn't want anyone to take you away from me!"

"Of course, you won't tell a soul. You won't be able to anyway."

The woman wanted to talk, but then she began to sway a bit. "Hey, I feel a bit sick." The drug was taking effect. Before Elina arrived, Ferenc put in a drug that would weaken her.

"As I said, you won't be able to tell a soul of our little arrangement. I was looking for someone to satisfy me tonight. What I want is blood." He then got a hold of my dinner knife and stood. Elina's eyes were filled with fear, and she ran towards the door, but he threw the knife on her back before she could. "Bingo." She yelped in pain and fell to the floor. Ferenc then got my hunting knife that he hid under the table and slowly walked to her. Elina tried dragging herself to the door and screamed for help, but the drug weakened her. "No one will help you, woman. This village is empty. I bought it for this purpose, to satisfy my urges. I love to rid of whores like yourself." Ferenc then kicked her head to the floor. She begged for her life; he got on top of her and stabbed her on the back of her neck.

She screamed and tried to fight back, but it was pointless; Ferenc kept at it. The crunches and blood made him feel alive. "What a feeling! I never wanted this to stop!" he yelled in ecstasy. Her movement stopped, and Ferenc stabbed her in the head one last time.

She was dead.

Her blood splattered on him; he took a deep breath and licked some of her blood.

Nenetl

Nenetl couldn't believe she was in Hungary; it almost felt like a dream. She was half Mayan and half white. Her mother was from a tribe in Yucatan, and her father was German who went to Yucatan to teach English and German. That's how her parents met.

Both fell in love with one another, and they lived together for a couple of months. However, her father's working visa would expire, and he never intended to stay in Mexico; he wanted his lover to go with him. However, she didn't want to leave; her father left, but he gave her his contact information just in case. After he left, her mother discovered she was pregnant with Nenetl.

Her mother raised her daughter, along with the tribe, but Nenetl was treated a bit differently from the tribe, some with admiration and some with distaste, especially the women. She grew up poor; her mother and tribe depended on tourists for income. When Nenetl turned fifteen, she received many proposals from the tribe's men but wasn't interested in any of them. The young woman had ambitions, and she wanted to be independent. However, there was a time when one suitor couldn't handle the rejection and tried to force himself upon her.

Nenetl fought back, and she told my mother. She knew her daughter would be in danger, so she called her former lover. As expected, Nenetl's father was shocked and angry that he wasn't informed about his daughter's existence.

The young woman hid in a hotel far from the village with the money she and her mother saved until her father picked her up. Nenetl's father was happy to meet his only child. He took her to his homeland in Trier, Germany; he was recently divorced. He and his ex-wife had no children. Nenetl was happy in Germany and learned the language, but she also knew Spanish and her tribe's language.

She kept in contact with her mother, but her mother wanted Nenetl to return since the man who tried to attack her left. Nenetl felt that she had more opportunities in Germany to work and send money to her. Her mother felt betrayed and gave Nenetl the ultimatum to return or never speak to her again. She chose the latter, and her mother never talked to me again. The young woman tried contacting her, but her mother refused to speak to her.

Her father was very supportive and told his daughter could stay with him as long as she wanted. Nenetl went to school and went to University with her father's help. She studied special education since she loved working with children and gained experience within the field. When she turned twenty-five, Nenetl decided to go to Yucatan to visit her mother; her father went with her. When they went to the tribe, they were informed that Nenetl's mother had married another man from a tribe; no one had heard from her since.

Nenetl stayed in Germany until she got an offer to work in a school created for orphaned special needs children. She couldn't let that opportunity go. Her father was sad but also proud of his daughter's success, motivating her to go. Nenetl promised him that I would call him and visit him. Now, she stood in front of the house she and her father purchased close to her workplace; she looked forward to her new adventure.

Training

It was morning; Nenetl looked at herself in the mirror. She was nervous as she didn't know what to expect. However, Nenetl knew that she had to be confident. If not, then what was the point of everything? Luckily, the orphanage was close by, and it was a twenty-minute walk.

She was ready and went on her way. As she walked, many people were going to work or doing chores. Many looked at her curiously, and some greeted her; Nenetl did the same. Twenty minutes went by, and she arrived at the orphanage. The orphanage was a modern-like building, and there were many windows. As Nenetl was about to enter, the doors were opened by an older woman.

The older woman looked to be in her late 50s. Her hair looked dyed in a bright red color, although some gray hairs were apparent. The woman had dark brown eyes. Her face had a lot of makeup that made her almost look like a clown. She was also a bit overweight but wore tight clothes.

Nenetl felt that the woman was trying hard to regain her youth. "You are Nenetl Kuhn, correct?" the woman asked almost roughly.

"Yes, Ms..."

"Call me Agnes. Come in; we've been expecting you." Nenetl did as she was told. Once inside the building, she had to admit that the interior was very decorative with the art projects that the children did. "For the rest of the week, it will be orientation and training; the following week, you will begin working with the children. You will also meet Mr. Ferenc Nadasy, one of the orphanage's creators. We have much to do."

Nenetl was shown around the orphanage, and it was decently sized. She saw many children waking up from sleep in the rooms she walked by. Her heart felt warmth for the children. However, she was sad that many of these children didn't have families. She promised herself that she would do her very best to teach and assist the children the best she could.

The young woman knew it would be challenging, but she was willing to take on it. She was taken to the meeting room where Agnes had her the training packets. Nenetl noticed that she and Agnes were the only ones in the room. It made Nenetl wonder if she was the only hire.

Nenetl focused on the training, which lasted more than two hours. She had to admit that it was not very interesting since Agnes wasn't enthusiastic. However, Nenetl focused on how to work with children, and to her, it seemed very basic, things she already knew. It made her wonder if any of the staff were truly trained. On the other hand, few countries consider special education necessary. That was when she knew that it was going to be difficult. She might teach others a thing or two, and they could do the same.

As the training ended, the door opened. The two women looked in that direction. Agnes immediately tried fixing her hair and hiding a blush on her heavily made-up face. "M-Mr. Nadasy, welcome, sir. We had just finished the meeting."

Nenetl looked at the man who had just entered. She remembered that Nadasy was mentioned in the paperwork, meaning he was the orphanage's creator. The young woman stood as he walked before her.

The two were face to face. Nenetl realized that he didn't say or do anything. To make the situation less awkward, she extended her hand out. "Mr. Nadasy, it is very nice to meet you, sir."

Ferenc looked uninterested as he saw Agnes, who was trying to fix her appearance. "What a pathetic cow. Who would want her at her age, especially with all that makeup and overweight appearance? She would be lucky to have a beta shmuck," he thought. However, his eyes focused on the other occupant. Ferenc wondered if she was mixed race. Usually, Germans were white, but the young woman had a light olive tone; he couldn't deny that she was beautiful.

The two stood in front of one another. Ferenc said nothing; he wanted to make her feel uncomfortable. He also wanted the young woman to know who was in charge. However, she did something he didn't expect.

"Mr. Nadasy, it is very nice to meet you, sir." She extended her hand out. Ferenc showed no emotion, but deep down, he was surprised. This woman made the first move; he looked into her eyes. Ferenc saw confidence and determination; he usually made people nervous and anxious, but she was the opposite.

He slowly got a hold of her hand; they shook hands. "You must be..."

"Nenetl Kuhn, Mr. Nadasy."

They let go of each other's hands. "Well, I am here to welcome you to this organization. This will not be an easy job. I expect the best from those who work for me."

Nenetl smiled. "Of course, and you will have it, sir."

He raised an eyebrow; he couldn't believe Nenetl had such confidence. "Alright, I want to see what you can do. You will provide us with a demonstration of what you know. You will work with some of the kids today."

Nenetl nodded and let Agnes motion her out of the room and to one of the classrooms. Ferenc didn't tell her that the children she would be working with had severe special needs. He didn't tell her because he wanted to break her confidence. "This will be fun, and I will see what she can do."

Nenetl knew that this was a test. The kids that she would work with were severe. A part of her wasn't amazed; she knew that many children who were severely disabled were quickly abandoned. Many parents in Hungary don't have the resources to care for their children and have patience. She was motioned inside a small classroom with two other teachers trying their best to help these children.

Many of the children are screaming or crying. Some of them are strapped in chairs from trying to escape. Other children are running around or jumping on tables. Nenetl could tell that the workers were already exhausted and stressed. Not many can handle working in this kind of field. She doubted that many who worked in the school were qualified to work with these children; many worked in this field for money.

She glanced at the window where she saw Ferenc and Agnes standing outside the classroom, looking through the window. Nenetl knew that Ferenc wanted to test her, but she felt something odd in his eyes. She took a deep breath and thought she had come too far to quit; she was determined to make this work. Nenetl introduced herself to the teachers; they looked relieved that Nenetl would help them. The young woman noticed that the classroom was in disarray; there wasn't any structure, which they needed. An idea came up, and Nenetl went to get some papers.

Meanwhile, Ferenc first saw how surprised the young woman was. "Is she having second thoughts? Will she quit?" he thought to himself. Many other workers weren't able to handle these children and left. He believed they were smart to go since they cared for their well-being. The only reason he made the orphanage was to gain the respect and trust of people so he wouldn't get caught.

If something were to happen where he was suspected of killing those women, he could use his influence and reputation to stop those suspicions. However, Ferenc was not worried since corruption was common in Hungary.

Now, he was curious about what this woman will do. He watched her walk to some cabinets, get some paper, and put them in the printer.

"What do you think she's doing, Mr. Nadasy? I hope that woman will not waste too much paper since it's expensive."

He didn't answer as he watched the young woman take out some printed papers; her eyes held confidence. Then, Ferenc watched her as she spoke with the teachers. All three of them put the children in their seats; some buckled and some not. The children were then placed in a circle.

Of course, many of them still screamed. The woman then got some soft, squishy toys and gave them to the crying children. That silenced them.

"Interesting. The other teachers couldn't even accomplish that."

Agnes was shocked that Ferenc completed Nenetl; it was the first time she ever heard him do such a thing. She bit her lower lip as she watched everything unfold; Agnes hoped Nenetl would fail.

Then, Nenetl put tape on the papers and posted them on the whiteboard. Pictures showed a figure washing their hands, exercising, working, playing outside, and more.

Nenetl then instructed one teacher to go to the sink, and the other would send two children to wash their hands at a time. It was very well thought out in Ferenc's view. Some children would try to run away, but Nenetl stood before them, did some sign language, and motioned them to do it. She wanted the children to learn sign language to communicate, leading to fewer tantrums.

"I can't believe it. This German was able to do it! Well, it's barely her first day; not every day will be like this, Mr. Nadasy."

"Quiet, go do your work. I will finish the rest."

Agnes reluctantly did as she was told, annoying cow. I watched as Nenetl and the teachers worked together to help the children. Some kids had tantrums, but Nenetl would find ways to calm them down. Feren couldn't deny it; he was impressed by her resilience as he observed her throughout the day. Under her leadership, she and the teachers put the children through nap time.

That was when Ferenc decided she would stay here; he had to know more about her to see if there was more than meets the eye.

Intelligence

N enetl stayed with the teachers until the orphans had their dinner. The young woman couldn't deny her exhaustion, but it was expected. A part of her was shocked that the teachers didn't know about working with special education children. Each country had a different education system, but she was happy that she could help and teach the teachers something new.

Nenetl noticed how grateful the teachers were. She promised she would teach them more before the working day, and they would make a teaching plan. Nenetl was about to help take the children to their rooms, but Ferenc entered the classroom. "Nenetl, I need to see you."

The teachers and Nenetl looked at one another, but the teachers thanked her and looked forward to seeing her tomorrow. Nenetl said her goodbyes as she exited the classroom and followed Ferenc. It was quiet between them as they went to one of the offices. Once inside, they sat and looked at one another.

"Nenetl, I must say that I was very impressed with how you handled those children. Germany seems to have good structures for handling children with severe difficulties."

"In a sense, Mr. Nadasy. I also did some studying independently; I'll admit that I was nervous when I saw the display."

Ferenc raised an eyebrow. "You did? Well, I shouldn't be too surprised; you froze on sight."

Nenetl giggled. "You are pretty observant, Mr. Nadasy. However, I used that time to observe the children and the severity of their disabilities. Many could agree that these children need fundamental structure; visual schedules greatly helped. Many of these children may not know or understand directions, but seeing what needs to be done helps them."

"I see, so you saw that in a short amount of time?"

"Yes and no. I also observed the classroom setting first to see if they had structure; when I noticed it didn't, I knew from that moment what was needed."

Ferenc's eyes never left Nenetl. He hated to admit it, but Nenetl was quite intelligent and observant. He had to respect her for it, even though she was a woman, in his view. However, Ference felt that she was too sharp and intelligent. It made him wonder if she could find out his true nature. He couldn't believe that he viewed her as a threat. "I might have to kill her," he thought to himself. Ferenc smiled. "I was wondering if I could buy you dinner? I want to hire you and keep you in this place fully."

Nenetl smiled. "I would be happy to stay here, but buying dinner is unnecessary, Mr. Nadasy."

Ferenc's lips were a bit wide. "Excuse me? You are refusing free dinner?"

The young woman blushed and looked away for a mere moment. "I feel that it's not professional, Mr. Nadasy. My refusal has nothing to do with you; I don't feel right about it. I only showed you some of what I can do, and the teachers here have been here longer."

Ferenc was surprised that Nenetl refused his offer. He was enraged but very impressed with her views; Nenetl was the first woman to reject him. "Very well, if that's how you feel, I will respect it. Either way, you had a little taste of what you will be dealing with. Do you still want this job?"

"Of course, Mr. Nadasy. I never expected this job to be easy. It would be an excellent opportunity to learn and teach my coworkers some strategies."

Ferenc nodded. "I agree; you hold the knowledge that could be very useful. Well, you are done for the day. I will come by tomorrow to see how your day went. I expect exceptional work from those who work for me." He stood up as did Nenetl; they shook hands and said farewells. Ferenc was left alone as he sat on his seat once again. His right hand trembled. His eyes then held no expression as he eyed the door. Ferenc felt she was a threat, but he also needed to know more about the woman. She rejected his offer for a simple dinner; many women would kill for the opportunity.

Yet, Ferenc knew that Nenetl didn't know how smart she was. Nenetl didn't realize she would have become one of his many victims if she had accepted his offer.

Victim #2

N enetl finally made it home after a long day; it was challenging but fun. After work, her coworkers invited her out to eat. The young woman didn't want to intrude, but the other teachers insisted. Nenetl relented and was taken to a family-owned restaurant owned by an older couple. She had a wonderful time with her coworkers as they asked her many questions about her personal life. Nenetl told them the essential things in her life; she knew not to make friends with coworkers since many could be backstabbers.

They all had dinner, but her coworkers paid for Nenetl's meal. She thanked them, and they all went their separate ways. Nenetl took a shower; when finished, she went to her laptop to write in her journal. As she was typing, her phone rang; it was her father.

"Hi Papa, how are you?"

"Mir geht es gut, Tochter. Ich habe mich gefragt, wie es dir geht. Wie war die Arbeit (I'm good, daughter. I was wondering how you were. How was work)? " asked her father.

"Etwas hart aber gut. Bei meinen Vorgesetzten habe ich einen guten Eindruck hinterlassen. Ich behalte den Job (A little hard but good. I made a good impression on my supervisors. I'm keeping the job)."

"I'm glad to hear that, Nenetl. You worked hard to get to your current position. Are you being safe?"

Nenetl smiled. "Ja, Papa. You worry too much. I can take care of myself. Besides, how is it with you?"

Nenetl and her father talked about their day until they were tired; they hung up. The young woman was tired, but before going to sleep, she turned on the television to see if anything was fascinating. There was nothing but stopped on a channel; she went to the restroom. The channel she stopped on was the news. Even though the news channel was in another language, it spoke about some breaking news. The newscast spoke about a missing woman who wasn't seen for days.

Meanwhile, Ferenc was in his usual hideout, eating some well-done steak with potatoes and artichokes on the side; he also had wine. He also was on his laptop looking at the current news; there was talk about the woman he had killed a couple of nights ago. He couldn't help but smirk; Ferenc felt proud of himself.

He watched as his victim's mother was crying about wanting her baby back; there was an award for any information. Ferenc couldn't help but chuckle at the mother's foolishness. "You will never see her again, fat cow."

Then, Ferenc heard a loud thud inside the room next to him. Ferenc paid no mind to it until he finished his dinner. While eating, he couldn't stop thinking about what happened during the day, Nenetl. He couldn't believe in admitting that Nenetl was strong-willed while handling those children. Ferenc gave her the most challenging children, but she overcame the struggle. He didn't know why he was looking forward to seeing her again. He shook his head as he finished eating his food.

Ferenc stood, turned off the television, and went to the other room; he opened the door. On the other side, a woman was on the ground with her hands and feet tied with rope. A cloth covered her mouth; she was screaming into it. He eyed the woman.

The unknown woman had short, curly, fake blonde hair. She was a bit overweight; the woman wore a short black dress that clung to her skin, making her large breasts pop out more. She had light skin with pink cheeks. Her eyes were dark brown; her face had slight wrinkles covered by heavy makeup. There were also a couple of moles on her arms and chest. To Ferenc, the woman tried hard but failed to appear seductive. He knew that she had very low self-esteem, which he found amusing.

He knelt in front of her, smiling. "Sorry to keep you waiting. I'm sure laying on the floor was very uncomfortable." The woman yelled onto the cloth; fear was in her eyes; it was something Ferenc loved to see, fear. He then took the fabric off; the woman yelled for help. "Oh, my dear. No one is coming. No one else lives here but me." Ferenc then went to a wooden cabinet and took out a knife. The woman screamed more as tears dripped from her eyes.

"Why are you doing this!? I have done nothing to you!"

"Why am I doing this? Good question, to get rid of worthless women like you. You only do damage to society with your selfishness. You're in this situation because you let your greed get you. Look what it led you." Ferenc slowly walked toward her. The woman tried to move away but couldn't move much of her weight.

Ferenc felt a sense of satisfaction and excitement as he watched the woman trying to escape, even though she couldn't. It gave him a thrill. Suddenly, he stepped on the woman's head so hard that her head hit the floor. "You have no one to blame but yourself; remember this as you die." Without warning, he stabbed the woman in the head with such force that it went through her skull, stabbing the brain.

The woman's eyes twitched along with other parts of her face as if her brain was losing control. Blood poured from her head to the floor; the woman was motionless. Ferenc didn't stop there; he got his knife out and stabbed her throughout her body. Blood splattered everywhere. Moments later, Ferenc stopped. The woman looked unrecognizable; a grave was dug for her outside.

Ferenc laughed as he was breathing heavily.

Invitation

N enetl woke up early to get ready to go to work. She felt excited to work with the children and co-workers again. The young woman showered and dressed. Nenetl looked at the clock, and it was 5 am. She had some time to go to the grocery store to buy groceries. To her luck, as she looked at her phone, a store nearby opened early, and off she went. The walk was short but relaxing. Nenetl saw some people doing some chores or getting ready to work. She got to the store and began some shopping. The young woman got many fruits, vegetables, and other healthy food with some frozen foods. She was done and walked home with bags on hand about an hour later.

Once home, Nenetl put the food in their place and relaxed for a bit, but eventually went to work. Nenetl decided not to cook herself lunch since she had little time. However, it would also allow her to try new foods. Once she got to work, some of her co-workers arrived, preparing for the day. Nenetl knew that they were waiting for her to express her ideas. She shouldn't have been too surprised since they had a hard time the previous day, but Nenetl didn't want to do more responsibilities.

It made her wonder if the teachers were fully trained. "Maybe I should ask Ferenc whenever he comes by," she told herself. The children were eventually woken up and got ready for the day. The children were calm, but not for long. However, Nenetl made a schedule to let the children know what was expected of them to do. Like last time, she asked her co-workers to get small groups of children in their charge, help them get dressed, brush their teeth, and take them to their seats.

Some children would try to give the teachers a hard time, but Nenetl would teach the teachers how to regain control. She knew that it was going to be a long day.

Meanwhile, Ferenc arrived at the orphanage. He was greeted by many of the workers, surprised by his arrival. Many of the female workers tried to get his attention. He would ignore them; it angered him that the women would try to be seductive. As he walked to Nenetl's classroom, he saw Agnes looking through the window. Agnes noticed Ferenc, and she fixed herself. "Ah, Mr. Nadasy, forgive me; I didn't know you were coming here."

"Is Nenetl in the classroom?"

"She's on break."

"I see. How's the situation with the children?"

Agnes let out a sigh. "Everything seems to be going smoothly. That new teacher seems to know to regain structure; even the teachers who worked here longer seem to follow her every command."

Ferenc could tell there was a hint of venom in Agnes' voice; she was jealous. He rolled his eyes. "Of course, she is jealous; Nenetl could do something she and these other worthless fools couldn't do." He decided to go to the teacher's lounge to meet Nenetl there.

Once inside, he saw Nenetl reading a book while drinking water. She looked up. "Oh, Mr. Nadasy. How are you today, sir?"

"Good enough; I decided to see how things are doing. From what Agnes told me, you seem to have control and stability over the children and staff."

"I wouldn't say that; I just have experience and used it." Nenetl looked away for a moment.

Ferenc noticed the hint of uncertainty in Nenetl. "If you have something in your mind, say it."

Nenetl cleared her throat. "Well, I do have some concerns."

"Is it another staff member?"

She shook her head. "No, it's the lack of training many teachers have."

Ferenc raised an eyebrow.

"I have to be honest; I'm a bit surprised that many teachers don't have the training in structure, behavioral control, and more."

"Your point is?"

The young woman felt that Ferenc was testing her. She had a hunch that he knew many teachers weren't qualified. "My point is that the teachers should be trained so they won't be overwhelmed."

The two were silent for a while. "Well, we don't have much funding for training. Also, many teachers don't have the patience or want to learn. Furthermore, many who applied for these positions are expected to have experience working with children. It seems they don't, and this is their consequence."

Nenetl was a little shocked at what she was told but felt that there was more to Ferenc than met the eye. Hungary did have its point of view, culture, and laws. "I understand, but weren't those who work under you the ones who hired them in the first place? Also, if those who are not qualified are chosen, it could lead to a disaster, especially for you, since you are the main one in charge."

Ferenc stood still. No one ever dared to say those things to him. He thought he would be angry, but to his surprise, he wasn't. He was impressed that she had the guts to tell him that to his face. Ferenc could have fired her or worse, but no. "You do make a good point. I'll tell you what. Let me invite you for lunch."

"Um, I-"

"I noticed you didn't bring any lunch. I can tell by your expression. Don't worry; it's a little cafe nearby. We can have more discussion about this situation. I will not take no for an answer. I expect you to be outside when it's time for lunch." With that, Ferenc left without letting Nenetl speak. He smirked to himself. "This will be interesting."

Cafe

I t was finally lunch, and the children would put on their beds for a nap. It was a bit tiring; many children weren't feeling well. Nenetl and the other teachers had to give them medicine and put them to bed. All teachers decided that a doctor would be called the next day if they weren't feeling better. However, when some students were taken away from the classroom to rest, the classroom went smoother.

It was lunch, and all the teachers went on their break. Some teachers invited Nenetl for lunch, but she remembered Ferenc's invitation; she had to decline. As the teachers went to the lounge, Nenetl noticed Ferenc standing by one of the doors; his hands were in his pockets. He motioned his head to her to follow him.

The young woman didn't know why but felt nervous. However, she gathered her confidence and went to him. "You look a little tired."

"Yes, many children were sick, but it was also an easy day."

They began to walk out of the building. "I imagine, when there are fewer children, it's easier to manage," said Ferenc.

"Of course." The two kept walking on another path where they could see several small buildings ahead. "So you said we're going to a cafe. Which one are you recommending?"

"Well, this cafe is owned by an old couple, and they have been given the teachers here discounts. However, they still follow the old ways of baking desserts and coffee, which gives it a natural taste."

Nenetl smiled. "Make sense; the old way of cooking and baking is more intimate and passionate. Unfortunately, many businesses care more about competition to get the next customers. It makes one forget how one truly lived and survived."

Ferenc was silent for a moment. He had to admit that Nenetl would take time to understand specific actions and things in life. Ferenc felt she was a little threat but couldn't help but feel intrigued. Nenetl was well-spoken, respectful, educated, and courageous. She wasn't like those women he had killed, dirty and worthless.

They made it to the cafe; the building was tiny and made of well-preserved wood. For Nenetl, it reminded her of a cabin in the woods. Inside was a fireplace with old-fashioned pictures of people and heads of deer. They were greeted by an older couple who motioned them to their little stand of desserts. Nenetl was amazed at the colors and smell.

Nenetl decided to order a piece of cake with coffee, while Ferenc ordered a Csoroge with tea. Ferenc paid for both of their desserts, even though Nenetl was hesitant. They sat at a table close to the window. "Thank you for this, Mr. Ferenc. Although, I could have paid for my own."

"Is there anything wrong with a man paying for a woman's treat?"

"Th-There's nothing wrong with that. It's just that I don't feel comfortable that anyone pays for the meal I can afford."

Ferenc chuckled. "So what would happen if you couldn't afford it? Would you still let anyone pay?"

The young woman shook her head. "I wouldn't go out in the first place. Many go out with others to see if they can get free food. Many use others to get what they want. I don't want to be associated with that. That's why I hardly have friends."

"I see. You do seem like a loner."

Nenetl let out a slight giggle. "It suits me fine. I work well alone and don't like to depend on anyone. How about you, Mr. Ferenc? You also seem to like to work alone."

He nodded. "I do; it's better that way. Many people wouldn't be able to handle me and live to tell the tale."

"I can see that; you do have an intimidating presence."

Ferenc eyed her. "You don't seem to be intimidated."

Nenetl could feel his gaze on her and his aura. "I was a little. Those who feel intimidated are the ones who don't have much confidence in themselves or know they can't get away from doing their little mishaps. If one is confident in their abilities, there is nothing to fear."

"She doesn't fear me since she feels very confident in herself." He mentally smirked. "We'll see how long it will last. Although, she has an interesting perspective. I haven't had an interesting conversation with a woman like this."

The two kept talking until fifteen minutes when it was time to return from lunch break. "Well, thank you very much for the dessert. I will pay next time."

Ferenc chuckled. "Oh, so you want a next time?"

"Well, you know what I mean. I want to pay you back for the dessert."

"No need. I have expensive tastes, and you wouldn't be able to afford it."

Nenetl was taken aback for a moment. "Understandable, but I can bake you something from my partial lineage. Anyway, have a good day."

Ferenc watched her as she went on her way. He had to know more about her and knew the one person who would give him what he wanted.

Ask

Nenetl made it home, and she was a little exhausted from work. It was not as bad, but the children's health worried her and the teachers. They were eventually given some medicine for the children; they got better. Tomorrow was Saturday, and Nenetl would relax. It was her chance to explore more of Hungary. "Might as well go on an adventure."

The young woman was cooking herself dinner until her phone rang. When she looked at it, it was a number she didn't recognize but still answered. "Hello?"

"Hello, Nenetl; forgive me for calling you so late. Is it a good time to speak?"

It was Ferenc. The young woman was surprised since she and Ferenc had gone to the cafe earlier in the day. She couldn't help but wonder how he got her phone number.

"If you are wondering how I got your phone number, it was in your paperwork. Now, I'm sure you're wondering why I'm calling you. Tomorrow is the weekend, and I wanted to ask what you planned on doing."

This caught Nenetl off guard. It seemed off that he would call her outside her working schedule to ask what she planned on doing. "I was planning on relaxing and exploring. Mr. Ferenc, is it appropriate for my supervisor to call me after work hours? I don't want to get in trouble or give people the wrong idea."

She heard him chuckle on the other line. "You shouldn't worry about what others think; I am the school's owner. Besides, I enjoyed our conversation and would like to know more about you. Since you're going to travel, I would like to tour the area briefly."

Nenetl felt confused. "I also enjoyed our conversation, but that isn't necessary, Mr. Ferenc. I would like us to keep professional boundaries of my respect for you. I am certain you are known and respected in the area, so I-"

"Miss. Nenetl. You don't need to worry about such trivial things. To let you know, I have a reputation in Hungary, and people wouldn't dare question my actions. I have done much for Hungary and other parts of Europe; my influence is vast. With that, I will be your tour guide. What time are you planning on traveling?"

The young woman wanted to let out a groan of annoyance. She wanted to explore independently and felt it wasn't right for her main boss to go with her. It didn't feel right. However, she worked for him, and the main reason for coming to Hungary was her position and experience. He also mentioned he had considerable influence in Hungary and other parts of Europe. Nenetl thought it wouldn't be wise to create tension for the issue. Also, it would be an opportunity to know him a little and to make a friend, in a sense. "I will be going at 9 a.m. since more people are awake."

"Perfect, I will meet you at the bookstore. Would you happen to know where it is? It is close to work."

"I didn't notice."

"I will send you the directions. I will see you tomorrow."

Ferenc hung up the phone. "That was plain weird. What is up with this guy?" Nenetl sighed as she continued cooking, but she would bring protective gear and let her father know her whereabouts for safekeeping. She had always done it in the past just in case something went wrong.

Meanwhile, Ferenc had just finished with the phone call; he smirked. He knew Nenetl was annoyed that he wanted to go with her for her little trip. It felt refreshing that someone didn't want to go out with them. It could become a bore of always being accepted. Nenetl seemed to have self-respect and wisdom. He wanted to go out with her mainly to know more about her and her weaknesses. He did view her as a threat since she was headstrong and intelligent.

Yet, it is satisfying to find a woman who was like that. He could have good conversations, leading to debates; he liked stimulating his mind. Ferenc couldn't believe what he was thinking. He was looking forward to going out with a woman, the gender he thought was worthless and vile. Yet, Nenetl seemed different. It didn't interest her when he told her he had much influence in other countries; she still wanted out of his little proposition. Even though he viewed her as a threat, he couldn't help but view her as a challenge, which excited him.

Ferenc then took out his phone and dialed a number. "Endre, I'm glad you answered. I would like you to look up some more information about a woman. I can pay you. I will also send you some of my paperwork on her." He hung up the phone.

Ferenc was alone in his study as he felt his heart beating rapidly. He had the urge to kill. However, he decided to refrain from killing women for the day. Tomorrow, Ferenc will be going out with Nenetl. Deep down, he hoped she would disappoint enough for him to kill her. Yet, another side of him hoped that she was different. He will find out eventually.

Bookstore

Nenetl woke up earlier than usual; she couldn't sleep throughout the night. All she could think about was Ferenc. The young woman felt awkward that she would be hanging around with her main boss, the owner, for Christ's sake! However, Nenetl calmed down and proceeded with her schedule to prepare for the day. She wore dark blue Levi pants, comfortable walking shoes, and a light brown shirt with a light brown jacket for the weather. Nenetl tied her long hair into a ponytail to avoid getting messy.

The young woman also packed some water bottles and snacks just in case. She was ready and decided to go to the bookstore where Ferenc wanted her to wait. To her luck, it wasn't far from where she worked. Many people began to wake up or do their daily chores. Many greeted Nenetl, and she greeted them back. She felt warm and happy that the people were open and kind; few would greet others.

She made it to the bookstore, and it was open. Nenetl looked at her phone; she was thirty minutes early and thought reading and checking some books would be nice while waiting for Ferenc. When the young woman went inside the bookstore, it was small with wooden walls with pictures, paintings, and animal heads. There were a couple of dance chairs in different parts of the buildings to sit and read. It gave her a comfortable vibe. Suddenly,

Nenetl saw an older man in his late sixties and bid her welcome. "Isten hozott, fiatal hölgy." (Welcome, young lady)

Nenetl studied the Hungarian language, but she wasn't as fluent yet. Luckily, she was able to understand the older man. "Üdvözlöm uram. Szép könyvesboltod van." (Hello, sir. You have a nice bookstore).

"Ah, your Hungarian is broken. Are you American?"

"No, I'm a German and Mayan. I was born in Yucatan, Mexico, but I lived with my father in Germany."

The older man looked surprised. "My word, it is so nice to see someone so mixed, especially a Mayan! Yet, you speak English pretty well. You learned many languages."

Nenetl giggled. "Yes, sir. You also speak good English."

"Well, I still have an accent. We do get tourists here now and then. I learned the language when I worked for an English company in Hungary, but I am retired and now own a bookstore to pass the time. Oh, where are my manners? The name is Levente."

"The name is Nenetl." The two shook hands. "Well, I'm here to kill some time. I am waiting for someone."

Levente raised an eyebrow. "Oh, is it a young man?"

The young woman cleared her throat. "Yeah, but we work with one another. He is just giving me a tour around the area, he insisted. Although, I would have preferred to go alone."

The older man laughed. "Oh, young people nowadays. What's his name?"

"Ferenc."

Levente stilled for a moment. "Are you saying Ferenc Nadasy?"

"Yeah, he's the one." Nenetl noticed how tense Levente became. "Sir, are you okay?"

He looked at her. "Where is he taking you?"

"He's only giving me a tour. I don't plan to go far with him; it would be too awkward."

"Don't go with him."

This confused the young woman. "To be honest, I didn't want to go with him, but he put me in an awkward position where it would be hard to refuse. I work in the school he made for special needs kids. He just called me so suddenly."

"Refuse his offer and go on your own."

Nenetl felt more confused. "Mr. Levente, what's going on? Would you happen to know Ferenc?"

Levente turned on the television and lowered the volume. "I don't know him personally, but I met him several times. He does have a reputation for being a rich man. However..."

"Yes?"

"There is something off about that young man. I feel that he has something hidden within him."

It was silent between them.

Nenetl sighed. "I felt something off about him, too, but I can't refuse him now. I gave him my word. However, I don't plan to be alone with him, so you have nothing to fret about. Now, are there any books you recommend?"

Levente bent a little under the counter and took out something. "Here, I want you to have this."

It was covered in a long handkerchief with some strings tied around it. "What is it?"

"A gun."

Nenetl's eyes became wide. "M-Mr. Levente! I-I can't accept this! I don't even like guns!" She tried to motion it back to him.

"It's for your protection, young one. Even though we barely met, I sense you are a strong yet kind woman. You came here alone, right? Sometimes, not everything or everyone is who they seem. It has bullets, so be careful. You can buy more at a gun store not far from here. The owner is an old friend of mine. Whenever you are in need, tell him that I sent you. Please, take it."

The young woman was still hesitant. However, he did have a point about her being by herself. It would be necessary to have a weapon to defend herself. "O-Okay, I'll take it. I still feel bad about it."

"Don't be, young one. It would be comforting to know you have something to help you one day."

Nenetl was about to answer but saw Ferenc's image through the television glass; he was outside the bookstore. He was waiting for her. "Well, I have to go. I wanted to read some books."

"Please come by again, young one. I do enjoy having some company."

"Of course, I might come again tomorrow to have a chance to read. See you soon."

Levente watched as the young woman left the bookstore and saw her with Ferenc. A chill ran down his spine. He watched them talk and then walk away. The older man ignored the television as the channel was the news. A dead body of a woman was found murdered.

Again

Police and forensic staff were at the crime scene. The crime scene was in the mountains. An officer stood as he watched the scene before him. The body of a woman was slowly being put in a bag. The officer was in his mid-40s. He had black hair with some gray hairs sticking out and a black beard in disarray. He wore a dark gray suit, a wrinkled white buttoned-up shirt, and some black slacks with black shoes. The man was overweight; his tired face had many wrinkles and slight acne due to the stress. He had slight bags under his dull brown eyes. The officer saw a female officer walking toward him.

"You look like hell, Elek. I thought you would be at home about now."

"I was supposed to, but I received a call about this case. You know how long I have worked in this kind of case, Kassandra."

The female officer was in her late twenties; her light brown hair was in a pixie-cut style with some red highlights. She had an average figure with some freckles on her pale face and chest. Her youthful appearance made her look almost childlike; many confused her about being an adolescent. Kassandra also has some small silver skull earrings. She wore a red buttoned-up shirt with the first couple undone, tight black jeans, and black boot-like shoes, making her have a goth appearance.

"So, who is the victim?"

"Well, there wasn't any identification or anything that would link us to her identity. The killer is pretty slick. He or she is trying to give us a hard time identifying their victim."

Elek walked forward and ordered the forensic team members to stop what they were doing; he wanted to see the body. He noticed many stab wounds throughout the body, and the victim's blood spilled throughout her clothes and skin. The young woman suffered a terrible death.

Kassandra knelt beside Elek. "This woman suffered a brutal death. Seeing the stab marks, the killer probably did this out of anger." She pointed at one of the marks on the body. "Look at this one. This cut was so deep that it made some marks on the bone." Kassandra looked at Elek, who watched the body quietly and intently. "Elek, are you not thinking about that again? You know how our boss hates it when you bring it up."

The older man stilled, looked at the body, and motioned the forensic members to complete their job. "I've seen this before, Kassandra. When I first began my job, my first case was of a teenage girl who was murdered. As time went on, I found bodies with the same memo. We have a serial killer on the loose. It's the same man."

"Come on, that was long ago. Look, if what you think is true, this killer has been killing since he was a teen."

"Correct. This killer has a hatred for women. There could be many reasons why he kills women, whether it be a hatred for his mother or he finds women weak."

Kassandra sighed. "Then, no women in the area are safe. We need to find out who this woman is. We need to get her description out in the news to see if anyone would recognize her."

Elek shook his head. "I don't think that would be wise. I have a hunch that the killer watches the news. He would probably stop momentarily or think of other ways to improve his skill. The killer doesn't want much publicity; he hides his victims, which means he didn't want them to be found." He looked at the young woman. "We need to find out who she is in secret. I have a friend who used to work in the forensic field in America and has more advanced technology. I can ask him if he can find anything about her." Elek went on his way while Kassandra watched.

She then looked at the body that was put in a bag; she sighed. "Thrown like trash, what a sick bastard."

Meanwhile, Nenetl and Ferenc walked around the area. Nenetl saw many stores and old houses built in the 12th century. She was surprised at how smart Ferenc was. He knew all about the history of the area. Nenetl was initially reluctant, but the more she was with Ferenc, the more she began to change her mind.

She learned a lot about the area. They would even stop at coffee places, bookstores, and more. However, the young woman would sometimes notice how the people viewed Ferenc. Many people looked at him with nervousness. It made her curious how Ferenc indeed was. It also made her wonder why people wouldn't look him in the face.

Was he hiding something?

Nenetl also remembered the gun she was given. She didn't tell Ferenc about it. The gun gave her chills, but it was good to have just in case for protection. Her thoughts were interrupted when Ferenc called out to her. "Huh? Sorry, what did you say?"

"Deep in thought?"

"Yeah, I was so entranced with the area that I felt like I was in the past. You're also knowledgeable. You made this day very exciting."

Ferenc chuckled. "Well, there is one place I would like to take you. If you're up to it."

"Sure, where?"

"It's up in the mountains; a historical monument exists there."

Nenetl felt awkward going to the mountain area with a man she hardly knew. She was about to answer when her phone rang. "Oh, it's my father. I forgot that he was going to call. I'm sorry, Mr. Nadasy. I have to cut things short. I have to speak with my dad. I'll see you next time." Before Ferenc could say anything, Nenetl went on her way.

Ference watched her walk away; he bit his lower lip until blood dripped. "She's escaped again. Again! What is it with this damn woman?"

Wonder

Nenetl was finally home but couldn't answer her father immediately due to a connection issue. She called her father back, and he answered. "Nenetl, I was worried about you since you didn't answer. Are you okay?"

"I'm okay, dad. I was taking a stroll and looking out at the area."

"Oh, that's good, and are you liking your job and new home?"

"Yeah, the people are nice. I might even have a new friend, an elderly bookstore owner. You know how much I like to read."

"That's true, and I would tell you to go out more often. However, I'm proud of you, Nenetl. You came out to be an intelligent young woman. By then, you might be able to visit?"

Nenetl smiled. "Well, I might be able to visit for Christmas. I asked for Christmas week off to be with you months in advance."

"Well, that will be great. I know you love going to the Christmas markets here. Well, I won't take up more of your time."

Nenetl shook her head. "Dad, you never waste my time. Besides, you called me at the right time. My boss was the one giving me a tour."

It was silent for a while. "Your boss was giving you a tour? Why would your boss do that? It doesn't sound professional."

The young woman mentally sighed. Her father was always protective since he discovered her existence and what was about to happen to her. Nenetl thought telling her father that Ferenc had given her a tour was a bad idea. "I thought the same, but my boss insisted. He just showed me around. He probably was being nice, that's all."

"Nice or not, I want you to be careful, Nenetl."

"I know, Dad. I am always cautious; if it makes you feel better, my new bookstore friend gave me something to protect myself. He reminds me of you."

"Okay then, I will call you by next week. If something happens, you know that you can always call me."

Nenetl smiled. "I know, Dad. I love you." The two stopped the call. Nenetl couldn't deny that she had a lovely time and was informed about the town and other cities. However, she would have preferred to travel alone. That was when she thought about Ferenc. Nenetl can't deny that he's good-looking, but something about him made him mysterious. There was also something off that made her feel uncomfortable around him. However, she didn't want to come out to be rude. The good thing for her was that she still had tomorrow off to have time for herself.

She hoped.

Meanwhile, Ferenc arrived home and slammed the door behind him. He punched the wall in the living room hard enough to make a small crack. He was angry. Angry that the phone call from Nenetl's father saved her life.

He had plans to take her to those mountains and bury her in the Earth. However, she escaped, even though she didn't realize what he was planning. Ferenc could kill any woman he wanted and could if given the opportunity. However, Nenetl escaped him not once but twice. He wanted to rip something to shreds.

Ferenc sat on the couch and contemplated what had happened that day. He intended to gain her trust and do what he wanted. History was Ferenc's favorite subject. People can learn from and make it, even ending their history. It was something comical to him. Nenetl listened intently and even asked him questions. Nenetl seemed to have an appreciation for history and cultures.

Ferenc stilled for a moment. His rage was dissipating, and he thought about the young woman. He felt she was cautious around him and didn't want to get too close. It made him wonder if she knew something was off about him. There was a possibility. However, he knows Nenetl didn't know who he was and what he had done. She better hope that she never does. It also made him wonder why she was able to escape him.

Also, Nenetl wasn't interested in him, even though he had looks, a high societal position, and money. She still wasn't interested. It made him annoyed and also impressed. She was probably the first woman who wasn't interested in him, more or less getting too close to him. It made him wonder if she was...different.

Was she a sign?

Was she going to be his match?

He doubted it, but there was something at the back of his mind that was telling him that there was the possibility that there was more to Nenetl than met the eye. Ferenc let out an annoyed sigh. Ferenc will try again to see if her blood will be spilled in his hands or if, by some miracle, she escapes his grasp.

If she escapes well, he must discover what makes her so special.

Levente

The weekday has gone by quickly, in Nenetl's view. It was a bit difficult since the kids acted up occasionally. However, she and the teachers worked together. She also felt it was tiring to always be in the lead. Many of the teachers didn't have the qualifications or much training. The good news is that everyone will get training by next week; it was a relief. Also, Nenetl was thankful that she didn't see Ferenc. She heard that he was in a business meeting all week. She felt that she could breathe easily and have more peace of mind. Nenetl didn't know why, but she was always cautious around him. He was handsome and had status, but something in her gut told her that he was not good news.

Yet, she didn't have to worry about him throughout the week. It was Friday, and her shift ended. Nenetl could always go home and relax, but it had been a while since she went to the bookstore. The young woman walked to the bookstore, and once inside, she didn't see Levente. Even when the doorbell rang, there was no response. The bookstore was dimly lit with some candles and old-fashioned light bulbs; it gave her a medieval gothic vibe. "Mr. Levente, are you here?"

No response.

Nenetl wondered if he went out; she didn't feel comfortable being in his bookstore if he wasn't present. She went to his desk to see if he was underneath, but when she looked over, he wasn't there. However, something caught her eye; it was a newspaper. In the newspaper, Nenetl read that a woman's body was found in an area not too far from this village. She raised an eyebrow. "Wow, I didn't hear about this."

Without her knowing that, someone behind her slowly walked toward her. A hand was extended and touched her shoulder. Nenetl squealed and turned. "M-Mr. Levente, you scared me!"

The older man laughed. "Oh, I'm sorry. I saw the opportunity, and I had to take it."

The young woman was slowly catching her breath. "Geez. I was looking for you. I didn't know if you went out. I was going to leave since I thought you weren't here."

"Oh, I was in the basement cleaning. Sorry I didn't hear you; my ears are slowly fading. It has been a while. How is work?"

"It's only been a week, but overall, work is good. Difficult but doable. I came here to read, maybe buy a new book to pass the time. Did you get anything new?"

Levente shook his head. "I will get new books by next month. However, I still have the old stuff. Sometimes, old minds and knowledge can be the good kind. So, how was your time with Mr. Nadasy?"

Nenetl went to a bookshelf while looking at the books available. "It was good. He was knowledgeable in history and made the tour fun."

Levente went behind his desk. He knew that she had noticed the newspaper. "That's good to hear. Was he pleasant to be around?"

The young woman shrugged. "He was okay."

The older man looked down at the newspaper and then at Nenetl. "Have you been hearing the news about bodies being found?"

"No, I don't watch too much television. I saw the newspaper; authorities found a dead woman's body. So what you are saying is that more have been found?"

"Yes, authorities don't want to say it, but everyone is saying there is a possibility of a serial killer."

Nenetl stopped and slowly turned. "A serial killer?"

"Indeed, many people are getting frightened, and the authorities are trying to keep hush about it. However, I believe that it will make it worse. I believe the public need to be informed about a serial killer on the loose." Levente looked down at the newspaper. "The woman was found in a place far from here."

"I see. That's a scary thought that one may be close to a serial killer."

"It is. The victims are usually women. Be careful who you hang around with, and do not go out too much at night. That's one of the reasons why I gave you the gun. You still have it, right?"

She nodded. "I was surprised that you gave it to me. Honestly, I don't feel comfortable having it. I don't like using guns."

Levente sighed. "I know, child. However, Hungary is still not an entirely safe country. Even though we live in a small town, it doesn't mean everyone here is a saint. Everyone has secrets. Also, be careful with Mr. Nadasy. He can be something else."

Nenetl got a book and sat on a chair. "I will. Besides, I'm not interested in him."

Levente went to the back of his bookstore to clean and fix some books. "Good because that man has intent in his eyes." He held a book about Elizabeth Bathory and put it on another shelf.

Questions

<hr>

Nenetl was walking back home and was happy to get some rest. She was going to think of some lesson plans for the kids. Maybe give some copies to the other teachers. Nenetl unlocked the door, and her home was dark. However, she felt that something was amiss. Nenetl turned on the light, and to her shock and horror, she saw someone sitting in the living room.

She screamed.

"Try to calm down; you might shock the neighbors.

Nenetl felt her heart beating rapidly from the surprise and shock. She was trying to regain her breathing. "M-Mr. Nadasy!? What are you doing in my home!? You scared me to death."

Ferenc sat on the sofa calmly; his eyes were unwavering. "I came by to visit. I have been having many meetings lately, and it was nice to have a break."

The young woman put her bags on the table but kept her distance. "So you decide to break into my home. You call this a break? With all due respect, this is concerning behavior."

Ferenc raised an eyebrow for a moment. He didn't blink his eyes; he stared at the young woman. He knew that she was being cautious as she should. "Your door was unlocked. I didn't want to sit outside because of the cold. Besides, you have nothing to worry about. You have neighbors around here."

It was silent between the two. "So, why are you here?"

"I would like to talk and perhaps invite you for dinner on Friday night. I know a special place that you have never seen before."

Nenetl was stunned. Ferenc wanted to take her out to dinner. "Mr. Nadasy, this is not appropriate. I also don't want my coworkers to get the wrong idea."

"It is professional, of course. It is nothing romantic."

The young woman still wasn't convinced. "I'm sorry, but I will have to say no."

Ferenc blinked. He sat still. She still said no. Nenetl refused him. "What if your job was on the line? You still would refuse?"

Nenetl walked behind the sink where knives were in a cabinet in case something happened. "Are you threatening me, Mr. Nadasy?"

The young man let out a slight smirk. "If you feel that way. I'm just asking a question."

"You wouldn't ask just any question unless it had a purpose. I'm not if you think I'm afraid of losing my job. There are many opportunities out there. I took this job not just for an opportunity but also to gain experience. I would still refuse if this dinner were just for a professional purpose. How is it fair that I would be the only one invited rather than the others? The other teachers have been working with the children longer than I have. They should have more of an audience than me."

Ferenc crossed his arms; his eyes didn't blink. His stare never wavered from her. He had to admit that he was impressed. It was difficult for him to be impressed by anyone. Nenetl didn't fully trust him, which annoyed him, but she also had self-respect and morals. She wasn't afraid to lose and walk away from everything. If Nenetl did decide to go with him, she would probably be his next victim.

However, she refused him. Ferenc knew he was good-looking and had everything a woman wanted to be a part of. He knew that Nenetl knew this. The female workers in the orphanage spoke about him and wanted him to choose them, even in secret. He could lure and kill them, but it would create more suspicion. He tried to feel Nenetl's blood, but his urge suddenly stopped when she refused him.

It was strange to him. "Why don't I have the urge to kill her anymore?" Ferenc had to know why. Out of all the women in the world, why was Nenetl different? He stood and blinked. "You passed my test."

This confused Nenetl. "Test? What test?"

"I have heard unsettling rumors about you. Word spread that you were trying everything in your power to seduce me, to get me to notice you."

"Rumors? I never heard about this."

Ferenc walked closer but stopped to keep his distance from Nenetl. He knew about the knives inside the cabinet she was close to. Nenetl was not afraid to fight back. "I am sorry, but your coworkers have been spreading these rumors. I know it is hard to believe, but they may act nice in front of you, but they let out their true nature behind closed doors. I don't mean this rudely, but women can be vicious creatures. They hold more jealousy and disdain toward their own sex. I wanted to end these rumors once and for all."

It was a little lie. However, Ferenc has heard the women gossiping about Nenetl. She helped them make their jobs more accessible, but they were jealous. Nenetl was a natural beauty and held more intelligence than they did. He also knew that word spread about him and Nenetl meeting outside of work. He knew Nenetl had morals and respect, but that didn't mean it would get her liked.

"Be it as it may. I'm not here to make friends. I am here to work and provide for myself."

"Good, as it should be. I know the way I came here is a bit bizarre. However, we do things differently in Hungary. My apologies. I will take my leave." Ferenc walked toward the exit and walked out of the house. Ferenc parked his car afar, ensuring it was not seen by Nenetl or others who might recognize him. Nenetl yet again saved her own life. She passed his final test.

It made him see that Nenetl was different from the other women he used to. He was assured that Nenetl wasn't entirely interested in him; it intrigued him. Now the next step was to learn more about her. Learn more about her personality, goals, family, and more. Maybe just maybe, it could lead to something more.

He stopped midway. "Why am I thinking these things? Why is this woman making me question myself? What are these emotions? Why can't I just kill her and be done with it? Do I really want to kill her?" Ferenc massaged his forehead. He had many questions and no answers. Yet, perhaps being around Nenetl, he would find out. At the moment, he had to try to earn her trust. He found a way and would put his plans into motion.

Advice

Nenetl woke up early in the morning; it was only 4:00 am. She knew that she wouldn't be able to go back to sleep. "Maybe I should go take a walk." Nenetly got herself dressed and walked out of her home. The sun wasn't fully set in yet, but there was fog giving the environment a hauntingly beautiful scene. Nenetly began to take a walk around the area with her jacket on. It was quiet, and some people we already awake while others were still asleep. Still, it was quiet, and Nenetl felt at peace. She walked two laps around the area and was going to go on her third lap until she saw someone familiar. "Mr. Levente, good morning."

Levente was sweeping dust out of his shop and stopped when he saw Nenetl. "Ah, good morning. I'm surprised that you're up early. You should still be resting to prepare for your job."

"Yeah, but I woke up and can't go back to sleep. However, taking a walk and clearing one's mind and body is nice. "You're also awake early. Do you usually clean your shop?"

"I do. It gets me something to do. I made some cookies yesterday. Would you like to join me for an early morning coffee?"

"If it's okay with you, I would like some tea. Coffee makes me moody for some reason."

Levente let out a chuckle. "Probably you can't handle the caffeine. Please come inside." The two walked into the shop, and candles dimly lit the interior.

"Wow, your bookshops feel medieval."

"It does. Candles can give a tranquil state of mind. Please, sit while I come with the tea and cookies." Nenetl sat on one of the chairs close to the bookshelves. She looked around and loved the feeling of peace in the bookstore. Levente was right, and the candles made everything feel tranquil. He arrived with a tray of two cups, a small glass of sugar and milk, and a plate of homemade cookies. Levente had a cup of coffee while he gave her the cup of tea. "I hope you don't mind Chai."

"Not at all. Thank you. The cookies look delicious." Nenetl got a cookie took a bite, and took small sips of tea.

"So, how is working coming along?"

"It's going good; I have good and bad days. I can express creative ideas to help the children and teachers."

Levente noticed the thoughtful look on her face. "Something else is bothering you, young lady. What is it? I know I shouldn't pry, but I learned that expressing one's troubles can help relieve them."

The young woman felt hesitant about speaking about what she was thinking and feeling, but Levente would have experience and knowledge on what to do in certain situations. "Well, Ferenc came to visit my home uninvited. I guess you can say he broke in. I doubt my doors or windows were unlocked."

The older man sat still as he almost put the cup of coffee close to his lips. He slowly put it down, and his expression became serious. "Did...Did he do something or say something uncomfortable?"

"Well, not necessarily. He wanted me to go out with him, but I refused. He told me that it was some test. Supposedly, my coworkers were spreading rumors about me."

"I see. This seems to bother you. Do you believe him?"

Nenetl looked down at her tea. "I-I don't know what to believe. At work, I am there to do a job, but at the same time, I do my best to help the other teachers make their jobs easier. He did mention that females tend to backstab their own sex. I hardly had female friends, but I heard many stories that having female friends isn't always beneficial. I was hoping it was wrong."

"Look, you are correct that you are there to work. You need to stop trying to please people. However, it would be best to let your coworkers work for themselves. Teach them what they must do and tell them they must do their jobs. You can't have all the responsibilities for yourself. They may not like it, but they choose to have those jobs and must handle the responsibilities. If they bug you, then report them or find another job. Life shouldn't be made this difficult."

Nenetl was silent as she took a bite of her cookie. "You're right. Sometimes it's hard to put oneself away from the problems of others."

Levente smiled. "Yes, it is great to be a good person, not a nice person. When you are nice, people will take advantage of you. When you are a good person, you keep your morals and values but know your limitations and when people are using you. Clear your position, and they will know who you truly are."

"Thank you for the advice. It was beneficial."

"It is no trouble at all. Please make sure not to get too close to Ferenc."

"I know. It was never my intention, to begin with. It seems that he is trying to get close to me. This is why people at work are getting the wrong idea."

Levente sighed. "Look, it is understandable if you feel uncomfortable around him, but you shouldn't have to deal with it. If it comes to the point where it becomes out of control, then find another job. I can help you in your search."

Nenetl stood up. "Thank you, Levente. I also appreciate the tea and cookies; they were delicious. I need to head out and be prepared for work."

"It is no trouble. Take some for a snack. Hope to see you soon. I will get some new books by the end of the week."

"Great, I will come by and check them out." Nenetl took two more cookies and walked out of the bookstore. He watched as the young woman walked away. He couldn't stop thinking about what she told him about Ferenc. He knew that things were only going to get worse. He stood up and went behind a counter when he saw the newspaper about the body they had found. No one was a suspect yet, but he couldn't shake off the feeling that the killer was closer than anyone thought. He met Ferenc several times but had a bad feeling about him.

He felt that Nenetl was in danger and it was best to call his good friend. He got his cell phone, dialed a number, and heard the phone ringing on the other end. Then, someone answered.

"Hello?"

"Hello, Elek."

Little Steps

Nenetl finally made it to work, and for the first time, she felt awkward. She couldn't forget what Ferenc had told her when he broke into her house. If what Ferenc said was true, how could she look at her coworkers the same? She helped them find new tactics to help deal with the children, and they would speak behind her back.

Yet, Nenetl wondered if Ferenc was lying. He broke into her house without her consent which was very creepy behavior. In her mind, Ferenc felt he had every right to do what he wanted; his actions and words are proof of that. That's one of the reasons why she didn't like or trust him. There was more to him that he didn't want people to see. Nenetl looked at her phone and arrived twenty minutes early. She thought it would be best to plan some lessons in the lounge. As she walked to the lounge, she heard talking. Nenetl stopped for a moment and noticed that one voice belonged to Agnes. She was speaking to other workers who were her coworkers.

She understood Hungarian since she studied it to work. "Are you all noticing Mr. Nadasy is paying attention to the half-breed? Why would he do that? She is not as pretty as I am."

"Like you have a chance with Mr. Nadasy. You're a single mother. Why would he want a woman with baggage when he can have any woman he wanted."

The two women argued. "Oh, shut it, you two. That bitch is getting his attention too much. I'm afraid she will eventually get a supervisor job," said Agnes.

Nenetl kept listening to their conversation. Ferenc was right; her coworkers were spreading rumors about her. She helped them when they didn't have the proper training and made their jobs easier. "You thought I was lying to you?"

The young woman flinched, and Ferenc walked behind her with a suitcase. Nenetl slowly looked at him. "Not entirely. As I said before, I'm not here to make friends."

"A thought everyone should have, but I can see it in your eyes; it bothers you. It bothers you that the coworkers you tirelessly helped make their lives easier go behind your back. Yet, you still try to act to be the better person."

"I am here to do my job."

"Indeed, but you have to worry about yourself. You are just expected to work together with your coworkers to help the children, but it never said that you had to train and make their jobs easier. I noticed you do more work during your time here than the others."

Nenetl said nothing. She hated to admit it, but he did have a point. Nenetl also hated that Ferenc was right all along. The young woman was always helpful but sometimes forgot that people would use others for their benefit. "You're right, but I think more about the kids than anything else. Part of my job description is to help the kids progress and help them with coping their environment. If I didn't help my coworkers, then it would make my job even harder; I wouldn't be doing my job."

Ferenc slightly raised an eyebrow. It annoyed him that Nenetl wouldn't fully accept defeat; she was stubborn. It annoyed him, but he couldn't deny that her fiery temper intrigued him. He knew she didn't fully trust him and wanted to learn more about her. He did promise himself that he would try to gain her trust. This was the best opportunity. "If you shall excuse me." He walked toward the lounge.

Once inside, the teachers and other workers talked to one another. When they saw their boss, they were stunned. "Oh, uh, Mr. Nadasy! Good morning, sir. We didn't think you would arrive today since you have a busy schedule," said Agnes.

Ferenc looked at everyone, and his stare made sure to let everyone know he wasn't pleased. "I'm sure you did. As I walked toward my office, I couldn't believe what I heard coming from your entitled little mouths. One of you is discriminating against one of the employees, Miss. Kuhn. Calling her a half-breed. Who was it?"

Everyone froze. Ferenc had an emotionless look, but his voice held a smooth venom. Many employees pointed to a young woman in her early twenties with long black hair that looked smooth and straightened. She wore makeup that made her face look tan. Her eyes were black. Her lips were slightly big, making Ferenc believe she had work done. She had a thin figure with a big bottom. "Plastic, that is all that she is. Pathetic woman!" He glared at her. "So, you were the one making racist remarks."

"M-Mr. Nadasy, I-I was making a joke."

"A joke? You know that I don't accept racist remarks in my organizations since we hire people worldwide. The work ethics of my employees represent not only the organization but also me. You dare make a mockery of me. You entitled spoiled brat?" The young woman trembled. "You're fired, and I will ensure that I will input the reason is racism. Now leave my presence."

The young woman began to cry and ran out. As she ran out, Nenetl hid in another room next to the lounge; she didn't want to be seen. However, she could hear everything about what was happening next door.

"Now, Ms. Agnes. Your behavior deplores me. You're an older woman who should know better than to be jealous of a young employee. You even went as far as to call Miss. Kuhn a bitch."

Agnes felt her face become pale. "N-No, M-Mr. Nadasy. I was speaking about someone else that is outside of the workforce."

"Oh, so you think I'm stupid? I heard everything that was being said in this room. I knew full well who you were talking about. Also, rumors have been spreading about me and Miss. Kuhn. You all wouldn't know who has been spreading these rumors?" No one said a word. "How pathetic you all have gone. You all can't stand seeing others succeeding because you refuse to work on yourselves. What kind of people have I hired? However, you all will have a strike and a last warning. If I hear another rumor or any discriminatory word from any of you, I will not hesitate to fire you all and make sure that I will put my reasoning why. Who would want to hire someone who pissed me off? Am I understood?"

"Y-Yes, sir."

"As for you, Agnes. As a supervisor and an elder, I am disappointed with your actions. I will not fire you, but you will be assigned to assistant supervisor. I will hire another to take your place. If you disagree, you are free to leave."

Agnes was shocked and wanted to argue, but she was paid good money that no other place would pay. She also had bills to pay. Not only that, she had a gambling addiction. The older woman couldn't afford to lose her job. "I-I understand, Mr. Nadasy."

"Good. Remember, you all have been warned, and I have many people on the waiting list for these positions. Good day to you all." Ference walked out of the lounge, and Nenetl wasn't there, but at the corner of his eye, he saw her hiding in another room next to the lounge. They glanced at one another. Ferenc gave her a quick wink and went on his way.

Nenetl was stunned at his sudden actions. She didn't know what to think.

Elek, the Detective

E lek finished making tea and carried a tray with two cups, a plate with desserts, and the teapot. He went to a few stairs that led downward; it led to a small hallway. There were small rooms, and at the end, the hallway led toward a medium-sized living room. "Thank you for waiting. Making certain teas can be difficult."

"There's no need to apologize, old friend. You always were a perfectionist. However, I see you have changed a bit."

Levente chuckled as he put the tray on the small table and handed his guest a cup. His guest put some sugar and milk; Levente sat down as he took his cup of tea. "Well, after working in the criminal justice for more than twenty years, one gets used to becoming a perfectionist. After retiring, I have lessened my expectations. How have you been, Elek?"

Elek sighed as he sat back on the sofa. "Tiring, but every day I have something new to do. I'm surprised that you decided to create a bookstore. Although, I shouldn't be too surprised since you always loved reading books in your free time. Do you have customers?"

"Now and then, but I wouldn't have it any other way. I gained a faithful customer who loves reading. Her name is Nenetl, and she is from Germany, but she is mixed. Intriguing young lady."

Elek took a sip from his tea. "Well, at least she brings you business. Anyway, you called me because you had a concern."

"I do. Even though I have retired from the line of duty, I still tend to be on the lookout to help you all out. I have been watching the news of a series of murders happening in different parts of Hungary."

The detective was silent for a moment. "Yes, however, we don't want to make this a hysteria. From what I gathered, many of these victims have similarities despite being small. Most of the victims were females of different ages and had similar backgrounds. Many were from poor or broken families. Some were escorts, and others were on dating sites."

"I see. The killer is trying to leave a confusing trail to confuse the detectives."

"It would seem so. However, this killer seems to kill women between 18-40. The killer knows that women from broken homes tend not to be missed. He thinks it would take longer to find the victims, or they would be bothered to be found."

Levente nodded. "So you think that the killer is male?"

"Yes. The manner many of the victims were killed, usually by stabbing. Many were stabbed more than thirty times; the killer has a hatred of women. Meaning that he hated his mother or a female family member."

The two men took sips of their tea. "Do you have any suspects?" asked Levente.

"My partner and I questioned previous criminals, but none matched."

"Well, I called you because I have been following the case and tried to do some digging. I do have concerns regarding a man." This caught the detective's interest. "Do you know a man named Ferenc Nadasy?"

This caught Elek by surprise. "Of course, he comes from a long line of nobility, and he is a businessman."

Levente finished his cup of tea. "What if I told you that there is something off about that man? He tends to be secretive and acts with disdain toward women."

"Hmm, as a businessman, he probably met with many women who would want him for his resources. It would be understandable that it could create distrust and hatred toward women. He doesn't have a criminal history."

"What if I told you that long ago, I saw him speaking to one of the victims."

Elek's eyes widened. "What!?"

"It was more than ten years ago, and he was creating the school—one time I've seen him speak to one of the female victims. Days later, she was never seen again; people said she probably left. I didn't think anything of it until I saw this." Levente pointed to a picture of a newspaper. The image was of a woman who was in her early twenties. "From what I remember, that young lady was rumored to be working as an escort for high-class clients. I believe she found out that Ferenc was building a school and tried to use the opportunity to her advantage. Unfortunately, she never returned."

The detective grabbed the newspaper; the murder case was always on the front page as new victims were found. Some have been dead for more than five years. "So what you're saying is that Ferenc Nadasy is a suspect."

His former colleague nodded. "Yes. I observed his behavior throughout the years; he's proud and secretive. His background would be the perfect cover-up if he were the culprit. Ferenc is popular, desired by women, and rich beyond measure. He could get away with murder."

"I agree, but we need proof to make him a suspect. If what you say is true, getting anything out of him would be difficult since he's wealthy. Remember, the Hungarian justice system can be corrupt when it deals with rich suspects."

"Then, it would be best to bring some corruption to light. The higher-ups will be pressured to heal their reputation; if they are forced to deal with a wealthy suspect, they will have no choice but to prosecute. We know people that can help." Levente ate a cookie. "I am telling you this because my main customer is working for Ferenc, and I am worried for her safety; I even gave her my gun for protection."

Suddenly, the men heard the store's bell ring. "Well, it would seem she arrived. It would be best if you met her." The men walked up the stairs to the store. Once there, they saw Nenetl. Elek couldn't believe that Nenetl was such a beauty. Even though she was beautiful, he felt a strong aura from her.

"Hey there, Levente. I came here to buy a new book for the week. I need something to read after another stressful day at work."

"I imagine. Nenetl, I want to introduce you to my good friend, Elek. Elek, this is Nenetl, my best customer."

The two looked at one another and shook hands. "Nice to meet you, Elek."

"Same here, young lady. If I may ask, do you work in the school owned by Ferenc Nadasy?"

Nenetl nodded. "Yeah, interesting place."

"Hmm. Nenetl, if you don't mind, please tell me about Ferenc." Elek didn't mean to be too upfront. However, he and his colleagues found more female victims and didn't have many suspects until now. Since Ferenc was brought up, Elek needed reasons to make him a suspect. If Levente's statement was true, he might need to use Nenetl to help him with his goal.

Suspicion

Nenetl was led to another side of the bookstore with a small reading room; she sat on the chair while the other men sat. Nenetl was asked about her boss, Ferenc; it made her curious and concerned. "So please tell me about Ferenc," said Elek.

"Ferenc? Well, one thing is that he is my boss and tends to be prideful. I think that's common for men with high status, right?"

"Yes, Ms. Nenetl. Mr. Nadasy does tend to be a prideful man. However, please tell me if you noticed anything odd from him."

This confused the young woman as she looked at Elek. "With all due respect, I feel that I'm being interrogated. Who are you really, sir?"

Elek and Levente glanced at one another and then at her. "You are intelligent, like Levente said. Alright, it's best if we don't beat around the bush. I am a detective, young lady."

"A-A detective?"

"Yes. Are you aware of the murders of young women in different parts of Hungary?"

Nenetl began to feel nervous. It was odd to her that a detective would be in the town. The sound of murder made her feel uneasy. "M-Murders? I heard some things from other people's conversations. I don't watch much of the news." That's when she remembered Elek's previous question. "W-Wait, why are you asking me about Ferenc?"

It was silent momentarily. Levente sighed as he massaged his head. He felt it was too soon for Nenetl to know the truth, but he didn't want to risk her safety. "Elek is trying to find suspects, and Ferenc is one of them."

"Wh-What?" Nenetl felt she wanted to throw up; her heart was beating rapidly. The shock was very sudden; her right leg was trembling.

"We don't want to lie to you, Miss. Nenetl. Many young women have been murdered for years and are believed to be linked to one person. Since this person has been doing this for years, we believe this person to have influence. I am not saying it is entirely Mr. Nadasy, but I am asking about some suspects we have." Elek knelt before her and smiled. "I know you are frightened, but I need to rule out suspects so the actual killer goes to justice. Believe me, Mr. Nadasy is not the only one I am asking about."

"Nenetl, please be honest with him. He only wants to know about Ferenc since you work with him."

The young woman was thoughtful. She remembered the first time she met him and until now. "W-Well, when I first met him, he was very proud. There were times when he asked me to go out with him or insisted on taking me to places even though I never wanted him to do. Also, there was one time when he..."

"Yes?"

"Once, he entered my home when I wasn't there."

The men looked at one another; Elek began to write some notes. "Did he do anything or try to do anything?"

"N-No. H-He wanted to invite me to go out with him. However, I did go out with him once in a small shop, and he wanted to take me somewhere alone; I refused to go with him."

This intrigued Elek; Ferenc's actions and behaviors made him suspicious. Ferenc seemed to be a man who didn't take no for an answer and always wanted everything to go his way. "Why didn't you want to go out with him?"

Nenetl wasn't expecting that question. Why didn't she want to go out with him? "I felt it wasn't professional for a boss and an employee to go out together. I don't want it to cause misunderstandings with the other employees. However, I couldn't help but feel a creepy vibe from him. I felt that he was a man of mystery and secrets. His actions and words made me not want to be close to him; he's also arrogant." Elek kept writing and felt he was getting a lot of information. "However, he told me that many of my coworkers were talking about me behind my back; he also defended me."

"How so?"

"Well, he told me my coworkers were talking about me behind my back. I thought he was lying, but when I went in for work today, I heard them saying racist remarks about me. He fired one of the workers and took disciplinary action against others."

"So he defended you, interesting. Well, thank you so much, Miss. Nenetl. I know this is a lot to take in, but I just want to rule out some suspects."

Nenetl stood up as she shook his hand. "So...what happens now?"

"Nothing at the moment. I have other people I need to interview in different areas. As previously mentioned that other suspects need to be interrogated. If anything comes up, I will call you, or you can call me." He took a business card from his pocket. "Here is my number. May I please have yours, just in case?"

Nenetl gave him her phone number. "I guess I'll leave now. Uh, Levente, do you have any new books?"

"The shipment hasn't arrived yet, but it will tomorrow. I will have them saved for you. Please don't worry too much about this, Nenetl. I am shocked as you are. Come by tomorrow, and we can talk about this."

The young woman nodded and left the bookstore, leaving the men alone. "Mr. Nadasy is a suspicious fellow; his actions alone are questionable."

"So what will you do now?"

"I am going to do more research on him. If he finds out that he is being suspected of murder, then he will do everything in his power to cover his tracks or worse. Well, I need to go on. Call me if something is amiss." The men shook hands, and Elek left the bookstore and went to his car. While walking in the car, he noticed someone standing afar in the village. When he looked, he saw a black vehicle parked afar, and although it was difficult to see through the tinted window, he knew it was a man. The car looked expensive, and that was when he knew that Ferenc was in the car. Elek entered his vehicle and drove off; he couldn't be seen much in the village since Ferenc was there. He also didn't want to endanger Nenetl, although he believed she was already in trouble.

Unexpected

N enetl finally arrived home and dropped her bag on one of the sofas where she sat. So many thoughts trailed in her mind; Ferenc was a murder suspect. She also thought about Levente and Elek; they were hiding something. Nenetl walked toward her room to one of the large cabinets by the door. The young woman opened the top shelf and took out the gun that Levente gave her.

She hated the feeling of a weapon that could take a life; she never took it with her. Of course, Nenetl worked with children, and she couldn't risk having the gun found and used. However, she hated the feeling of it since it brought chills down her spine. Yet, it made sense to her why Levente gave her the gun; he knew something was off with Ferenc. The young woman sat on her bed, holding and looking at the gun. Then, it dawned on her that if Ferenc was a murder suspect, she or anyone in the town could be the next victim.

"Oh my god..." Memories flooded her with all the times when Ferenc asked her to join him in private to certain places and when he entered her house without her permission. It was as if Ferenc knew what he was doing; he had to have experience. Her thoughts were interrupted when there was a knock on the door. Nenetl slowly walked toward the living room and took a peek from one of the windows from afar; it was Ferenc. She felt her blood turn cold; she tightly gripped the gun and contemplated what to do. "I can pretend that I'm not home, but he's not stupid to fall for something like that," she told herself.

The young woman put the gun behind her pants and over her long sweater, walked toward the door, and opened it. Ferenc stood on the other end with his hands over his pockets. "Hello, Miss. Nenetl, may I come in."

"S-Sure. I'm surprised that you didn't break in." Nenetl wanted to slap herself for saying such things; she was nervous. She was scared but knew she had to keep her composure and think about what to say in the worst-case scenario. "S-Sorry, I went a bit far." Ferenc entered as he looked around the house and stood silently. "Would you like to sit? I can make coffee or tea or give you something else to drink."

"That won't be necessary; I don't plan to stay here long; apologies for returning unannounced."

Nenetl shook her head. "No, not at all. I-I wanted to talk to you about what you did at work. Why did you do what you did? I mean, I didn't want to cause trouble in the workplace."

Ferenc slowly turned to look at her; his hands were still in his pockets. "No, the workers caused their problems. They knew what was unacceptable, but they still took the risk even though you helped gain control over the children."

Nenetl was trying to play it cool; she was thankful she had something to discuss. "Still, I feel that everything may not be the same."

"Nothing stays the same forever; change must happen so times can progress. Anyway, I saw you in the bookstore and saw an interesting man coming out. Would you happen to know who he is?"

This is what the young woman feared. Her heart was racing, and she was thinking about what to say; she didn't want to put Levente at risk. "N-No. When I got to the bookstore, I-I just heard the owner and this man speak." Ferenc slowly walked closer to Nenetl, but she stayed in her place. She didn't want Ferenc to think that he could intimidate her. Nenetl didn't expect Ferenc to see Elek walk out of the bookstore. "I can't let him know what went on."

"Really? Would you happen to know what they were talking about?" he asked in a whisper-like tone.

"M-Mr. Ferenc, what is going on with you?"

"You sound nervous."

He suspected her of hiding something, and Nenetl knew she was hiding something. "Yes, because this is not the first time you have come here unannounced, Mr. Nadasy. I feel scared because I feel that something is going on. I don't want to get involved in something I am not a part of."

Ferenc was expressionless; his eyes didn't blink once as he looked at the young woman. He tried reading her expression, and he eventually gave her more space. "Forgive me, I have been stressed as of late, and since I am known in the country, I have enemies everywhere."

Nenetl felt relieved that Ferenc believed her, but it could have been a ruse to make her mess up. "Oh, I can't imagine your responsibilities, Mr. Nadasy. Either way, thanks to you, these children can get an education and a roof over their heads. We also have our jobs, thanks to you."

"Indeed, I came here to invite you to dinner. There's a special place I wanted to take you."

Fear overcame Nenetl. Even though there wasn't proof that he was a killer, she didn't want to go anywhere alone with him. "Th-Thank you for the offer, but I don't want people to get the wrong idea. I don't want people to think that there is something between us. H-How about this? You can come here at 7 pm, and we can do an outdoor dinner."

The businessman raised an eyebrow. "An outdoor dinner?"

"Yes, well, I call it that; it's like having a barbecue. When I lived with my mother and tribe, we used to cook and eat outdoors as a community. We used to have bonfires to cook food and eat under the night skies and stars. Have you ever done that before?"

"No."

Nenetl's eyes widened. "Well, this will be your first time. It may be simple, but I always find it soothing to eat with Mother Earth since she has given us plenty to live off of. Yet, we can be selfish and take more than what can be offered. What do you say?"

Ferenc thought what Nenetl said was ridiculous but couldn't deny feeling intrigued. He never experienced something like that before. "Very well, I will come by tonight."

"Great! Can you bring some sodas? I can buy the meat since you are my guest."

"Sodas?"

"Yeah. You have drank sodas before, right?" When Ferenc said nothing, Nenetl couldn't help but feel stunned. She had never heard of someone never trying soda, but he was wealthy and probably had the best quality drinks. "Well, you can buy simple Coca-Cola or anything that interests you. I can also make some salads to go with the meat. Would that be okay?"

He nodded. "I will see you tonight, and I will bring sodas."

"Perfect! See you tonight!" she motioned him out of her house and waved goodbye. When he left, she went inside and closed the door shut. Nenetl drooped down to the floor, thinking about what she had done. However, it was better than going out with him to a place that could be her timely end. For now, she had to play it careful and safely, hoping that everything would go well.

Barbeque Pt.1

Ferenc was driving toward Nenetl's home with the sodas in the back of his trunk. He never did his shopping since he always hired someone to do it for him. The businessman thought it was beneath him. When he went to the store, he saw many people staring at him and pointing at him. Many women went to him, wanting to take a picture with him, but he had to 'politely' refuse. Ferenc had to keep up the facade; he hated the lot of them and wanted to spill their blood.

Anger filled in his being that Nenetl asked him to do a simple chore. However, he was the one who accepted the invitation. He still wondered why he accepted in the beginning. He made a left turn as he made his way to the village. The more he thought about it, that was when the businessman realized that he wanted to do something he had never done before. His family never went to a barbeque, much less outside. During childhood, Ferenc heard other classmates mentioning that they and their families would go camping or have barbeques. He squeezed his driving wheel when he remembered his parents, especially his mother.

His mother inherited the Bathory bloodlust and inherited the family's insanity. His mother was an influential figure in the business world, and everyone respected her. Everyone had no choice since she was ruthless and had no problem dealing with all those who went against her. Her husband was a second cousin who didn't have much influence and feared her. He let her do what she wanted while he did what he wanted. Ferenc despised how weak his father was as he let him and his siblings suffer at the hands of their mother.

Ferenc bit his lower lip so hard that it bled; he stopped when he got to Nenetl's house and turned off his car. He looked at his reflection and licked his blood away until he noticed a light that came from the back of Nenetl's house; it looked like a fire. He got out of the car and got the bag of sodas, a Coca-Cola, and Traubi. When passing through the fence, Nenetl appeared from the backyard with some first on her hands. "Oh, M-Mr. Nadasy, you arrived."

"You said 7 p.m. or am I mistaken?"

"No, you're right on time. I just finished fixing the bonfire; the food and salads are ready. Please come through here while I wash my hands." Nenetl undid the hose by the garden and washed her hands while Ferenc entered the backyard. When he did so, a scent hit his nose; it was one of the most delicious scents he had ever smelled. Once in the backyard, he saw a bonfire lit with wood and coal. What intrigued him was that something was close to the fire, covered by banana leaves. Meanwhile, Nenetl finished washing her hands and was nervous but had to act natural, or Ferenc would suspect her, knowing that he was a possible murder suspect.

She dressed in a simple jeans t-shirt with a handmade sweater above, while Ferenc dressed to impress. Nenetl felt he was trying to convey that he was above others, and she couldn't blame him since he was raised in a certain way. Nenetl walked to her backyard, where she saw Ferenc standing by the bonfire, looking at the food she cooked. She put plates of food on top of small boulders. "Thank you for bringing the sodas; I have cups so I can-"

"No need, I bought some. What did you cook?"

"Oh, I cooked the usual potato salad, guacamole, pico de gayo, rice, beans and the Mayan dish called Cochinita Pibil."

Ferenc looked at her. "What is that? I never heard of it."

"It's pork with pibil, a juice of a Seville Orange and annatto. That distinct orange color comes from the annatto, and other than the heavenly smell, it makes it instantly identifiable. After the pig is marinated, it's wrapped in banana leaves and placed in a pit with coal at the bottom. The coal essentially smokes and pressure-cooks the meat as the entire setup is covered with dirt for a few hours while it cooks." Nenetl smiled as the scent hit her nose; it reminded her so much of home. "This is a popular dish within the tribe I lived with. Please take a seat." She motioned him to sit on a log close to the fire.

The young man looked at the log and scrunched his nose. "You want me to sit there?"

"Yeah, the point of a bonfire and barbeque is to eat and be a part of nature. Our ancestors have done so for centuries. Sometimes, we forget the old ways, and we shouldn't lose it. However, I can get a blanket so you don't have to-"

"No need, I will sit." He motioned her to the bag of cups and sodas, which she took. Ferenc slowly took his seat while looking at the fire. "Now, my pants will get dirty, this damn woman! I should have-" Ferenc wasn't able to finish his thought when he saw Nenetl open the banana leaves, which exposed the sizzling Cochinita Pibil. His eyes widened at how delicious it smelled and how cooked it was. He had tasted and seen many delicious foods in high society, but this was on another level. The meat looked so natural.

The young woman got a plate and served salad, rice, and beans, and then used a knife to cut the pork, which she put on the plate. She got a fork and gave the plate to Ferenc. "I hope you like it. What soda would you like?"

"Either," he responded while holding the plate. Ferenc didn't realize that his mouth was salivating, something he wasn't used to. He cut a piece of meat and tasted it. His eyes widened; it was the most delicious meat he had ever eaten.

"Do you like it?" Nenetl asked while handing him a cup of soda.

Ferenc took it and took a sip; the Coca-Cola also tasted delicious. "It is. I'm surprised that something like this can taste delicious."

"I'm glad. Food tastes better when it is cooked naturally; it can take a while, but it is worth it." She smiled while serving herself a plate but glanced as Ferenc put guacamole on the meat and ate more. Nenetl felt relief that he at least liked the food but knew that she wasn't out of the woods yet. "May I sit next to you?"

"I am not that narrow-minded. This is your home, and I am but a mere guest."

She did just that, and it felt bizarre and nerve-wracking to sit next to an influential figure who may or may not be a murder suspect. Nenetl hoped that she would make Ferenc lose interest in her, but her gut told her she may not get what she wanted.

Barbeque Pt.2

Nenetl ate her food peacefully and was relieved that everything was going smoothly between her and Ferenc. What surprised her was that Ferenc ate three plates of food. She always had imagined that men like him watched how much they ate to keep their appearances. Whenever Nenetl watched him eat, Ferenc ate with delight and passion; he was enjoying the food she made. There was still some food, and once they finished eating, they sat in front of the bonfire. "Sorry for saying this, but I noticed you ate three plates of food."

Ferenc glanced at her. It was true that he ate at least three plates of food, which was something he never did. Whenever he went to extravagant parties, he ate one plate of food. It was something of a customer in the upper class. Many upper-class individuals cared about their appearance. Even he cared about his appearance and was careful about what and how much he ate. However, Nenetl's food was delicious and flavorful, and he couldn't help but eat more than intended. From all the food he ate, Nenetl's cooking was by far the best. "Yes, I have. Is that a problem?"

"Not at all. I'm happy that you ate as much as you did. I was afraid that there would be more leftovers. I was afraid that you wouldn't like my cooking."

"I'm not used to saying this, but the food you made was superb. Do you know how to cook many recipes?"

Nenetl smiled as she took a sip of her soda. "Well, I know how to cook a lot of Maya and German recipes since I grew up in both cultures."

"When I first read your paperwork, your last name sounded German, but when I first met you, I was surprised to see that you are of mixed descent. It is not very common here in Hungary. Tell me about your homeland and culture." The young woman didn't want to tell him about her life but didn't want to be rude. She told him about how her parents met and how she got to Germany. Nenetl ensured not to give out too much information. She didn't want to risk him using any information against her. It was silent when Nenetl finished talking. "Your mother seems to be a controlling and selfish woman."

"Well, I was her only child, and she didn't want me to leave, so..."

Ferenc chuckled. "Sometimes one doesn't want to see the bad side of one's parents. Your mother may have protected you from a forced marriage, but she did it for her gain. Your mother feared losing her one source of companionship, control, and power. Your mother was good at hiding it until you grew older." He noticed that Nenetl looked confused and upset; it was something he liked to see. However, it looked as if Nenetl was willing to listen to his explanation. People would usually scream or try to fight back against the argument. He was impressed that she was keeping her temper. "Your mother was born and grew up in a patriarchal society; women had little power in such communities. The only power women have in these situations is with their children, and they try to have them in their clutches. When their child grows older, it threatens their power when the child decides to leave. Your mother didn't respect your wishes so she did what she did."

It was silent between them once again. Ferenc wanted to hear and see her reaction; he enjoyed the power of getting a response. Nenetl nodded. "I never saw it that way. It could be true, but I may never know what my mother thought. I forgive her either way."

The businessman's excitement dissipated when he didn't get the desired response. "Damn, this woman! Why doesn't she act like her sex!?" Ferenc looked at the fire. "You would forgive your mother? Why? She abandoned you and left you for another possible family that she made?"

"What would I gain with anger and resentment? I gain nothing but contempt for her and life. If I focused on that, I wouldn't live as I wanted. I can't deny that she saved me from a forced marriage and raised me the best she could. It's also because of her that I have been allowed to meet my father and have all the opportunities I have. That is enough for me."

Ferenc kept looking at the fire. He didn't know how or what to respond. After learning more about her personality, Ferenc realized that Nenetl was not easy to break. The businessman bit his lower lip and finally admitted that he would never be able to break Nenetl. He could take her now and kill her, but what angered him was that he had no motivation or the need to do so. He was silent, thinking why his urge to kill wasn't overwhelming him when he was close to her. The businessman stood. "I will take my leave. Thank you for inviting me for dinner."

Nenetl also stood. "No problem. Would you like to take some food for tomorrow? It's a little too much for me."

"If you would let me have some." He watched as she cut pieces of meat and put other food on plastic plates. A part of him needed to see more of her, to be more with her. He realized that he had the urge to be close to her. That's when he thought about an idea. "I invite you to come with me to Diósgyőr Castle, a public museum, and very popular at this time of the season."

The young woman stilled as she finished putting the last piece of meat on Ferenc's plate. She knew that Ferenc would not leave her alone. She feared being close to him since he was a murder suspect. She feared that the outcome could be costly if she kept rejecting him. He could have killed her if he wanted to, but he didn't. Yet, it allowed her to determine whether or not he was an actual killer or not. She could help the authorities. "O-Okay. I never heard of the castle. What time would you like to go?"

"In the morning since it can get packed. Don't worry, there will be workers in the castle and I need to check on it since there will be festivities held there."

"Oh, you are a very busy man. Are you sure you want me to go? I mean, you are busy and-"

"You invited me here, so I want to invite you. I will not take no for an answer anymore. I will pick you up at 8 am." Ferenc got a hold of the plate of food and went off his way, leaving a stunned Nenetl behind. The businessman got into his car and put the plate of food on the other seat. He sat in silence for a moment and thought about the event. Ferenc had to admit that he had a good time. He never would have imagined that something so simple could be so enjoyable. Now, he would have more time to be around Nenetl to see more of her personality. How she was at work could have been different than how she was in her private life. She wasn't like other women who wanted to know what he had; Nenetl was private and mysterious.

With that, the mystery about her excited him, motivating him to do everything he could to solve it. When Ferenc turned on his car, he realized something he never thought he would admit. Since Nenetl didn't care about his position and wealth, he finally accepted that he might have found an equal. He drove off to think of his next course of action.

The Plan

The clock was ticking at night, and Nenetl found sleeping difficult. When she looked at her phone, it was 11 p.m. Ferenc's invitation plagued her mind, and she was frightened of the possibilities that could happen. Elek and Levente scared her with the chance of Ferenc being a suspect of murder. She didn't want to be a victim, but there were times when innocent men were put into prison for crimes they didn't commit. Nenetl, however, also had the urge to find out the truth, even with the possible danger.

The young woman sat up from bed. She put on a jacket and some tennis shoes and walked out of her house. Nenetl couldn't wait until morning since Ferenc would pick her up early. She had to talk to Levente and get his help. Her footsteps were the only thing that echoed in the small village; some people were already asleep or closing their stores. When arriving at the bookstore, Nenetl knocked on the door; she waited. Nenetl felt terrible for waking up her older friend but was entrapped in a situation she never asked for. She waited without response; Nenetl knocked on the door with more force.

About a minute later, Levente walked toward the door wearing a dark brown robe. He turned on the lights to the bookstore as he massaged his eyes. Levente looked annoyed, wondering who would be insane enough to knock on his door. At first, he thought it was a possible burglar, but to his confusion and surprise, Nenetl was on the other end. The elder slightly opened the door. "Jó ég (Good heavens)! Nenetl, why are you up so late!? You scared me half to death!" He was slowly regaining his breathing from the nervousness, and when he calmed down, he noticed her look. Nenetl looked nervous and frightened; he knew it was not good news. "Come inside, I assume we have a lot to talk about."

Nenetl entered the bookstore and let Levente lead her to another door, leading her to a large room with a full-sized bed, a small kitchen, and a bathroom in one. There was one cabinet, one small wooden table, and a chair. It amazed her that Levente could live in one room where he could do all his necessities in one go. However, it looked organized and clean. Levente motioned out the wooden chair to have her sit. "Sorry, there is not enough room; I cannot be far from my business."

"It's no trouble at all. It looks as if you keep everything organized. I like it."

"Would you like some tea or anything to drink?"

She shook her head as she sat on the chair. "No thank you. I don't plan to stay for long, but there is something I need to tell you and to get your advice in."

Levente sat on his bed and crossed his arms. "This is about Ferenc, isn't it?"

"Y-Yeah, it seems he was spying on us when Elek visited. After I left and returned home, Ferenc came by unannounced. He asked me who the detective was. I had to lie and change the subject as fast as I could. He is smart enough to know when I am lying or not." Nenetl sighed as she scratched her head. "I-I was so nervous that I invited him for a cookout."

This surprised the older man. He would never have imagined that a man with such status would do something so odious as having a cookout. "And he accepted?"

"He did. I cooked for him, and he brought sodas; we talked, and he invited me to the Diósgyőr Castle tomorrow morning. I-I came to you to see what you think I should do. Should I change my mind?"

It was silent between them; Levente was thoughtful about the situation. He couldn't believe that Ferenc was smart enough to spy on them. However, it made sense to him since Ferenc seemed interested in Nenetl. "Could it be that he is developing feelings for her?" Levente shook off the idea. If Ferenc were the serial killer, then he would be psychopathic. Psychopaths tend to lack emotions and aren't likely to form relationships. The older man wished Elek was here to see what he would do in this situation, but there wasn't much time. That was when he made a decision. "Go out with him. If you don't, he will immediately suspect you know something about him. He knows that we're meeting up and that Elek is involved."

Nenetl dreaded the response but also anticipated that it would be his response. "I-I thought so."

"Look, we all are involved in this, whether we want to or not. I believe that he won't do anything to harm you. He had the opportunity to do so when you invited him to dinner. You interest him."

"Wh-Why? He's a powerful businessman who could have any woman he wanted. I am a nobody."

Levente sighed. He felt that Nenetl didn't realize that there was more to her than met the eye, and Ference saw that. "Ferenc is curious about you; probably not many people made him feel that way. I know you didn't do it intentionally, but he is complicated. He won't be easy to eliminate, no matter what you do. So go with him and try to figure him out."

"Figure him out?" Nenetl's eyes widened. "Wait, you mean...?"

"Yes, you will keep an eye on him and any kinds of behaviors he displays. If something is amiss, then tell me so I can inform Elek. If Ferenc asked you about Elek, then he is hiding something."

He noticed Nenetl becoming uneasy. "So, there is a possibility that he might be...?"

"I don't want to lie to you anymore. I have always suspected something to be off from him. I know you feel it from him, too. It must be true if our gut tells us something is wrong with a person." The feeling of dread overcame the young woman, so much so that her body slowly began to tremble. Levente went to her and put his hands on her arms. "Calm yourself, Nenetl. I'm sorry if I scared you, but I also don't want to keep things from you. You and I are a part of this. As I said, Ferenc will not hurt you, especially since you are known here, and he is seen with you. He won't do something so foolish."

"O-Okay, I will go." Nenetl stood up. "Levente, what happens if he doesn't leave me alone?"

The older man sighed as he massaged his eyes. "If the situation worsens, you will have to return to your home country. If I were you, before leaving with Ferenc, call your father and tell him where and with whom you are going. Also, take the gun I have for you, just in case. Understand?"

"Okay. Good night and sorry for waking you up so late."

Levente nodded as he showed her out the door; he watched her walk into the night and back to her house. "It's getting worse than I thought. I can't help but feel that this is only the beginning of something big. Nenetl might have to leave this country."

Call

It was finally morning, and Nenetl was up and awake early. She only slept for three hours after she went to visit Levente. She couldn't stop thinking about today's events and couldn't help but be scared. The young woman didn't want to eat or drink anything because of her mixed emotions. It was 7:35 a.m., and she thought it was a good time to call her father. Nenetl dialed the phone number and waited for her father to pick up. The phone from the other side rang, and it eventually stopped.

"Hallo (Hello)?"

"Guten morgen, Papa (Good morning, dad)."

"Ah, guten morgen! Wie geht es dir und wie ist der Job, Tochter (How are you and how is the job, daughter)?"

Hearing her father's voice made Nenetl feel at ease. Her father always made her feel safe and protected, but since she was going with Ferenc, she didn't know whether or not she would arrive home alive. Nenetl squeezed her phone tightly. "No, I will come home alive," she whispered.

"Hast du was gesagt (Did you say something?"

Nenetl got out of her thoughts and was about to respond, but then she saw a car parked outside her home. Ferenc arrived; it was 7:45 a.m. Nenetl bit her lower lip, thinking he arrived too early, but she felt it wasn't bad. It would be a good idea that he should see that she was speaking to her father. "Entschuldigung, ich habe über etwas nachgedacht. Ich gehe heute mit jemandem auf ein Schloss (Sorry, I was thinking about something. I am going to a castle today with someone)." She saw Ferenc getting out of his car and walking to the front door of her house; he knocked on the door. The young woman slowly walked to the door and opened it.

Ferenc was on the other end, and he wore a long black coat with a white buttoned shirt with the first three buttons undone. The bottom of his shirt was tucked in his black khakis; he wore clean black shoes. His hair was slicked back and clean-shaven; Nenetl could smell his soft cologne. Ferenc raised an eyebrow when he saw Nenetl speaking on the phone. She smiled and motioned him to enter, which he did so.

"Du gehst mit jemandem, etwa zu einem Date (You're going with someone, like a date)?"

Nenetl noticed Ferenc looking at her as if he was listening to her conversation. Since Ferenc was a businessman, she wondered if Ferenc understood German. She knew she had to be careful on what she spoke of. "Es ist ein freundschaftlicher Ausflug. Ich fahre bald los und wollte sehen, wie es dir geht. Vielleicht rufe ich dich an, sobald ich zurückkomme (It's a friendly outing. I'm heading out soon and wanted to see how you're doing. Maybe I will call you once I return)."

"Gut, ich warte auf Ihren Anruf. Liebe dich (Good, I will wait for your call. Love you)."

"Ich liebe dich such, papa (I love you too, dad)." The two hung up, and Nenetl was now focused on Ferenc. "Sorry about that. I haven't spoken to my dad in a while and I promised that I would call him a while back."

Ferenc nodded. "We should get going before the traffic gets bad." He motioned her outside. Nenetl got her bag, which contained the gun that Levente had given her. She didn't want to use it, but it made her feel safe. The two left the house, where Nenetl closed and locked the door; she was motioned to walk and get inside the car.

Once inside and the car door shut, Nenetl closed her eyes and took a deep breath, hoping she would come home alive. Ferenc got into the driver's seat, turned it on, and drove away from the house. They drove past many houses; they were getting close to Levente's shop, and once there, Nenetl saw Levente getting out of his shop. The older man noticed the car and the two of them, and he was expressionless. Ferenc eyed him but then kept his eyes on the road. "He's up early."

"Yeah, it would seem so. He's probably opening his store."

Ferenc drove off from the village onto the main road. "Yet, he doesn't make many sales; you are his best and only customer."

Nenetl knew that Ferenc was trying to test her, but she refused to give him the satisfaction he wanted. "Even if I was his only customer, at least he gets one. It doesn't seem to faze him; it goes to show that Levente has a stronger will than most who start a business and give up."

"I tend to agree but to keep a business afloat, one must get profit; it is the way of the business world."

"I know, Mr. Nadasy. Yet, he can still keep his business afloat all this time. One shouldn't judge a book by its cover." Nenetl noticed he glanced at her quickly; she smiled as she looked toward the window. It was quiet between them, and they drove by many parts of the woods until they finally got to the city. "I want to thank you for coming yesterday. It was nice to have company."

Ferenc was still quiet. "You don't have friends and yet you refuse many of my invitations."

"Yeah, I'm a bit of an introvert. I imagine that you have many friends."

Friends. It was a foreign concept and word to him that he believed was for the weak. "I never had friends."

"R-Really? With all due respect, how can someone like yourself not have any friends?"

"Just because they were born or earned wealth doesn't mean they will always have friends. I can say that the more money you have, the less friends you have. Many people want what others have and will pretend to be something or someone they are not. It's difficult to trust anyone." Ferenc couldn't believe what he had just said. Never would he say something about friendship. He didn't care since he thought friendship was a waste of time since they weren't forever. However, Ferenc never had one and didn't know what it felt like to have one.

Nenetl slowly looked at Ferenc, who was entirely focused on the road. "Wow, I always that that the wealthy always had everything easy. To some extent, it is true, but I imagine how lonely it can be when one doesn't have someone they could at least trust. To me, that's a life not worth living for."

Ferenc didn't know why, but her words irked him. "Is she trying to say that my lifestyle is imperfect? This blasted woman doesn't know how many people wish to be in my position." However, the more he thought about her words, the more she mentioned not having anyone to trust. That was when he realized that he never had anything he trusted, not even his family. Did he know what trust was? Ferenc didn't know what it felt or what any other emotion felt.

Pain was his only comfort.

The other emotion he began to feel was curiosity. Curiosity toward Nenetl, she was the only one who started to make him feel...something. He made a left turn toward a stone-made bridge, and he then parked in the parking lot. Ferenc heard and noticed Nenetl gasp in amazement. "Welcome to Diósgyőr Castle."

Diósgyőr Castle

Although the stone walls looked worn out, Nenetl couldn't believe Diósgyőr Castle's beauty. She always found old castles magnificent and fascinating since she loved history. Outside the castle were a few white tarps; people walked in and out of the gates carrying chairs and tables. That was when Nenetl remembered that Ferenc mentioned festivities were going to occur. When she and Ferenc walked toward the castle, many workers stopped and greeted their employer.

Nenetl noticed that the women eyed him with lust and wonder; they watched her with disdain and jealousy. "Oh, if you desperate women knew about the suspicions of this guy," she thought. Ferenc stopped, as did she, when she noticed an overweight man coming their way, but he wasn't alone; another man was with him.

"Ah, Mr. Nadasy. I am so glad that you arrived."

Ferenc let out a small smile. "Gerson, it is good to see you again. I see that everyone is preparing for tomorrow's festivities. Although, I see that they are barely starting." His smile slowly dissipated. "I hope that they will be able to finish for tomorrow."

Gerson laughed nervously. "W-Well, of course, Mr. Nadasy. We were short-staffed, but then my new assistant got more workers. Everything will be done by 8 pm, so you needn't worry. By the way, let me introduce you to my assistant, Boris Farkas. The young man looked to be in his early twenties to early thirties. Boris was six feet tall with warm-beige skin, a broad face, and a slightly muscular build, making him look like a model. His brown-blondish wavy hair was tied nicely with a few strands loose; his eyes were blue. He wore a white buttoned shirt with a black undershirt beneath. His clothes almost clung to his muscular body, which would make any woman salivate at the sight of him. Nenetl couldn't believe how handsome he was. "My god, he's even better looking than Ferenc." However, not much of his looks caught her interest; it was his smile. Boris' smile looked and held a sort of innocence that was almost rare. In Nenetl's view, his smile would make anyone feel at ease.

"Mr. Nadasy, it is an honor to meet you in person. I admire all your work, and you motivated me to study business." Boris motioned out his hand; Ferenc looked at him and shook his hand.

"Well, it is nice to motivate others." He let him go. "I expect nothing less from those who work for me."

Boris nodded and then looked at Nenetl; his blue eyes were on her momentarily. "Who might you be, Miss?"

Nenetl was brought back to reality and composed herself. "Oh, uh, I'm Nenetl Kuhn. I-I'm just Mr. Nadasy's worker. It's a pleasure to meet you." She motioned her hand to him, which he gladly took; they shook hands. However, they still held hands while looking at one another.

Ferenc noticed the scene and slowly got annoyed. "Gerson, Boris, take us inside and show us the status of the preparations."

"Of course, Mr. Nadasy. Boris, please lead the way. Since you will one day take my place, it would be befitting that you would do the honors." Boris and Nenetl let go of each other's hand and Boris motioned the group to follow him inside the castle.

Once inside, the castle's center had many tables, chairs, and a large stage. Some pillars and walls were decorated in red and black fabrics, and some roses were the same color. While Boris explained the designs and what was to be expected, Nenetl slowly separated herself from the group while marveling at the castle's interior. The castle wasn't as big as other European castles; Diósgyőr Castle was only two levels, with many rooms.

Nenetl was so busy marveling at the castle that she didn't realize Boris finished speaking about the preparations. Boris noticed that Nenetl was looking at the castle's interior and felt intrigued. "It seems, Miss. Nenetl is enjoying the sight of the castle."

Ferenc turned to see Nenetl and let out a small huff. "Indeed. You planned everything thoroughly, Boris. However, such praise will be given once the festivities end."

"I expected that, Mr. Nadasy. I assure you that everything will go perfectly and to your expectations."

"Um, excuse me." The men looked at her. "Is there a restroom? I need to go bad."

Boris smiled. "Of course, Miss. I will show you the way. If you would follow me." He motioned the young woman to follow him. Ferenc eyed the duo walking further away; he didn't know why, but he didn't like that Nenetl willingly went with another man.

Meanwhile, Boris led Nenetl to a slightly dark hallway far from the castle center, and at the end, there were two doors, which were the restrooms. "Here you are. I will wait for you here."

Nenetl nodded as she entered the women's bathroom and did her business. When finished, she washed her hands while looking at her reflection in the mirror. She was relieved that there were people in the castle, which meant Ferenc couldn't do anything to her. Yet, he still had to take her home, but she doubted he would harm her. When leaving the restroom, Boris stood by the wall, waiting for her. "Are you ready to go back?"

"Honestly, I really would like to look around the castle alone. Would it be possible?"

"Unfortunately, you can't go alone since there are restrictions." Boris smiled. "However, since I have some authority here. I can give you a small tour, but it has to be quick since there is still some work to do."

Nenetl smiled as she felt her heart beat rapidly. "I would like that."

Boris

- -

Boris led Nenetl to a path of stairs when he opened a door by the end of the hallway. He entered first as Nenetl followed. "Could you please close the door behind you? We can't have people know that we're breaking the rules."

Nenetl gently shut the door as she followed the handsome young man upstairs. "Are you sure that you still want to do this? I-I don't want you to get in trouble with your boss."

"It's quite alright. Gerson is an understandable man, and he trusts me. Besides, you are an important guest; I could tell you're a history buff. Do you know anything about this castle?"

"No. Do you also like history?"

The young man smiled. "I do. I'm doing my Master's degree in history and business. I will be done with the program by the end of the year, and when that happens, I will apply to become a Professor at Eötvös Loránd University."

"I heard about that university. I heard it is one of the best in Hungary. Do you go to that particular university?"

"No, I attend the University of Szeged but am pretty ambitious. I want to gain experience teaching. My dream is to create my own tour company and show the beauty of Hungary's history." Boris got to the end of the staircase and waited for Nenetl. "Although, Hungary also has its dark side like all countries do. You could say that I want to help my country prosper."

Nenetl couldn't help but admire Boris' dream. She thought that he would be stuck up due to his good looks. Sometimes, she met good-looking men, and many were conceited and vain; Boris seemed different. However, she wanted to be cautious since people can put up a facade. The two walked in a hallway out in the open, and they could see the lower level where Gerson and Ferenc were. Boris then began to speak about the castle's history. It was first built in the 12th century but was destroyed during the Mongol invasion of 1241-42. After the invasion, the castle was rebuilt and held significance for King Louis the Great.

As Boris explained more of the castle's history, Nenetl would look around and touch the castle walls. It brought her excitement and peace that she could touch a historic building. The young woman also felt at ease when she was close to Boris. He held a different aura than Ferenc. She felt that Ferenc was arrogant and lacked empathy and understanding. What made her nervous, besides that he was a murder suspect, was that he was very secretive. He ensured that no one could read him or know much about him. Boris wasn't afraid to speak about himself and what he wanted to achieve.

Meanwhile, Ferenc was listening to the plans for tomorrow's festivities and getting bored. He wanted to leave and have some time for himself and with Nenetl. He would glance to see if Nenetl would arrive, but nothing. What the businessman hated the most was that he was getting impatient that she and Boris were taking too long. The thought of them being alone for too long irked him. Gerson noticed Ferenc's annoyed expression. "Mr. Nadasy, does something trouble you?"

Ferenc looked at his phone. "Nenetl and your assistant are taking too long. How far are the restrooms?"

"N-Not too far, Mr. Nadasy. I am certain that they will return soon."

The businessman looked around, and when he looked at the castle's upper level, he saw them together. Boris looked as if he was showing Nenetl different areas of the castle. Ferenc also couldn't help but notice Nenetl's smile. She looked like she was having a wonderful time with another man. He didn't realize that his right hand was made into a fist and that he was trembling. "Call your assistant."

Gerson wasted no time as he called out to Boris. Boris and Nenetl stopped and looked down at the two men. Boris sighed. "Well, our tour has come to a close. I hoped to tell you more about the castle." He motioned her to walk back toward the staircase. "Anyway, I hope you enjoyed the small tour I was able to provide," he said while walking down the stairs.

"Yeah, I did. You make history even more interesting."

"Will you be here tomorrow night's festivities?"

Nenetl shook her head. "I wasn't invited and I'm not much of a party person."

Boris stopped and slowly turned toward her. "I was wondering if I could take you to one of my favorite cafes tonight. I will be busy all day tomorrow, and I have school responsibilities. Tonight is my only free time this week. Even after the festivities, I have to help clean up, make plans for other festivities, do homework, and more. I would have more of a free schedule next week. What do you say?"

The young woman was surprised that Boris would ask her out in such a short amount of time. A blush made its way to her face, and she couldn't help but turn away. "Are you sure? I mean, we just met, and you're busy."

"Are you dating Mr. Nadasy?"

"N-No, of course not! He just wanted to show me this castle! I-I work for him!"

Boris chuckled. "Well, then, there is no harm going out. Besides, it's just to get to know each other. We both like history, so we have that in common. You intrigue me; there is more to you than meets the eye. Also, aren't you a little curious about me?"

Nenetl was astounded by how blunt Boris was. She slowly looked at him; his eyes never left her. He held confidence that many men nowadays didn't have. It made her feel attracted to him. "O-Okay. I-I guess that would be fine."

"Perfect. Can you give me your number and I will text you the address where we should meet. I am sure you wouldn't be too comfortable for me to pick you up yet." The two got their phones out and gave each other their numbers. Boris texted Nenetl first, and she received the message. He then sent her the address of the location where they would meet. "Well, come on, we must get a move on."

The duo made it to the end of the staircase, and once they were out, they were surprised to see Ferenc on the other side. Nenetl shivered violently. Ferenc looked calm and collected, but his eyes told her another story; they were filled with rage.

Threat

The three were silent as they looked at one another; Ferenc's eyes were on Nenetl, who shivered. When seeing his eyes, there was a hint of anger, and it made Nenetl frightened of what he would do. "Mr. Nadasy, sorry for taking so long, it's just that-"

"Ms. Nenetl here was curious to know about this castle's history, and I wanted to show her around. I take more responsibility for this."

Ferenc's stare never wavered; he never once blinked. "So, you wanted to show her around the castle, eh? Is it also necessary that you two switch phone numbers?"

Nenetl's fingers fidgeted; she tried to contain her composure, but when glancing at Boris, he didn't look nervous. "Yes, since we both have an interest in history, we wanted to speak more on different history topics. It doesn't hurt to make friends, Mr.Nadasy." Boris's eyes never wavered when looking at Ferenc. Nenetl couldn't help but think it was brave of him since he didn't know what was happening with Ferenc and what he was suspected of.

A smirk slowly came across Ferenc's lips. "Well, I'm afraid that is not appropriate. You see, Miss. Kuhn will be my date for tomorrow's events."

"E-Excuse me, s-sir?"

"You heard me, Miss. Kuhn. You will be my date for tomorrow."

This made the young woman mortified. She didn't want to be Ferenc's date. He could have any woman he wanted, but he chose her. She wondered if he had something sinister planned; not knowing terrified her. "I-I didn't know you wanted m-me to be your date, Mr. Nadasy. I-"

"You and I are going. Boris, I will entrust you and your boss to take of everything. Do not disappoint me." Ferenc motioned to Nenetl to follow him, which she reluctantly did. Before going down, she and Boris looked at one another. The young woman wanted to tell him that everything was a misunderstanding. She said that she didn't want to go with Ferenc. However, Nenetl didn't want to put him at risk; she didn't know what Ferenc could do to him. To her surprise, Boris looked unbothered; he smiled at her.

Nenetl and Ferenc were downstairs and walked out of the castle. They then walked toward the car, but Ferenc stopped before the passenger door. "M-Mr. Nadasy?"

"Delete his number."

"Ex-Excuse me, sir?"

He slowly turned and faced the young woman with an unreadable expression. "Delete his number. What you two are doing in unprofessional."

She didn't want to delete Boris's number and believed Ferenc was getting too much in her personal life. "Sir, I believe what Mr. Boris and I are doing has nothing to do with being professional. We work in different trades. Besides, I would like a friend since I am still used to this country."

Ferenc slowly walked toward her; Nenetl wanted to stay on her spot to show he had no power over her. However, when he didn't show any signs of stopping, the young woman slowly walked back but stopped when hitting a street pole. Although Nenetl wasn't looking at him, she could feel his eyes were straight at her. She never met someone who held so much power and intimidation. "You refuse to do what I say?"

Nenetl knew that Ferenc always got what he wanted, but she didn't want to fear him. He also had no right to say what she had to do with her private life. That was something she refused to accept. "Mr. Nadasy," she said while slowly looking at his intimidating eyes. "Wh-Who are you to say what I should do personally? Wh-What you are doing is unprofessional."

The businessman stilled. She called him unprofessional. He also noticed that she was looking up at him with determination and fear. "What did you say?"

"I-I said that what you are doing is unprofessional, sir. Wh-Why should I delete the number if it is not affecting my work? Mr. Boris and I work in different professions; we just want to know more of one another." That was when Nenetl remembered Ferenc's comment. "A-Also, you said that I was your d-date, even though I wasn't asked."

"Yes, it is because I did need a date for tomorrow's events, and I believe that you would be a great candidate."

The young woman squeezed her hands together; she felt he wasn't honest with her. She knew that Ferenc would never tell her the truth since he was too proud, and he didn't want her to know who he indeed was. "A-Although I appreciate being thought of as a good candidate, I still wasn't asked. Also, I-I am not fond of parties."

"I am not fond of parties either. You said you wanted friends and to know the people of this country, well this is your opportunity. I will not accept no as an answer. If you refuse, then..." Ferenc smirked, "...I must relieve you from your position."

A gasp escaped Nenetl's lips. "Wh-What!? You can't do that! That is illegal and-!"

"Perhaps in Germany, but here in Hungary, we have different laws, and no one cares. Of course, if one pays a good amount."

Ferenc admitted that corruption was involved and that he wasn't afraid to bribe those in power. Nenetl should have seen it initially and realized that Ferenc must have experienced bribing politicians and other country leaders. She was powerless, but Elek and Levente were on his trail to try to prove that he was a...serial killer. He seemed to have some interest in her. Why else would he want her to delete Boris's number and want her to be his date? Then again, she did want to help prove whether or not Ferenc had another facade. "Who has been acting unprofessional, Mr. Nadasy? Why are you doing all this?"

It was something the businessman couldn't respond to. He was usually prepared for anything and to destroy anything that came across his path. However, Nenetl asked him the most simple yet complex questions. He didn't know why he was so angry that she and Boris exchanged numbers and why he wanted her on a date. All he knew was that he had an interest in her and a solid need to be by her. "Whatever you feel doesn't matter. You still work for me and have what you own here in Hungary because of me." His smirk widened; it almost looked sadistic. "Now, you are in my playground, Nenetl. I am not used to not having what I want. What I say goes. Now, you will go with me tomorrow, and I will not take no for an answer."

His true colors were slowly coming out to the surface, and Nenetl knew it. Ferenc was slowly letting out his true self. However, even the most powerful man always has a weakness. He liked a challenge; it gave him a thrill. If she just gave in, the game was over, and she could end up in a worse situation. "Very well, but only this once. You are right, Mr. Nadasy. Everything I have here in this country is because of the position you have given me. Then perhaps my calling is not here. I might as well return to Germany and find a new path." She let out a small smile, trying to show bits of her strength. "I am a woman of my word, Mr. Nadasy. I will go with you but I still do not appreciate my employer to mind in my personal life. If you want to fire me, then go ahead. I still appreciate all that you have done for me."

Ferenc's smirk died down as he felt rage that Nenetl didn't quiver beneath him. She was willing to leave if need be. He knew that she thought that she had an advantage, but he refused to be defeated. "Very well, Miss. Kuhn. I shall take you home." He motioned her to go to his vehicle, where he opened the passenger side. Once inside, Nenetl let out a quick, deep breath as she watched Ferenc walk around to the driver seat. She knew that she was off the hook but didn't know how long she could keep it up, and if she would survive to help Elek and Levente,

Victim #3

The drive back to the town was quiet and intense, especially for Nenetl. She tried hard to look away from Ferenc, but her curiosity made her want to look and ask him many things. However, his threats echoed in her mind; she didn't want to push her luck. However, Ferenc would keep his eyes on the road but take glances at her. He couldn't believe himself but couldn't help but be enamored by her beauty. The businessman always looked into a woman's beauty; he believed he deserved only the world's best.

Why would he deserve something beneath him, he would always ask himself. He was so used to women hiding who they were that he had almost forgotten what a woman with natural beauty looked like. The more Ferenc looked at Nenetl, the more he thought about what was reality. The businessman viewed Nenetl as a trinket who needed to be possessed and caged so the rest of the world wouldn't gaze at her beauty.

Like how Boris looked at her, the memory of being close and smiling at one another made his blood boil. No one was allowed to receive her smiles except him. He squeezed the driving wheel as he hated that it bothered him so much. Ferenc could drive to a desolate area and kill her to make his thoughts go back to the way they were, but he couldn't.

He didn't want to.

The duo eventually arrived in the town, and Ferenc parked in front of Nenetl's house. "We arrived."

Nenetl immediately undid the seatbelt and tried opening the door, but it was locked. Her body tensed, but she refused to look at Ferenc. "May you please unlock the door."

"Do you have a nice dress to wear for tomorrow?"

"I-I have a few, but I don't know if they are up to your standards. I'm certain that you have certain expectations," she said in an almost challenging tone.

Ferenc noticed how she spoke, and he knew she was annoyed and upset; he smirked. He enjoyed messing with people's emotions. However, Nenetl acted calm, cool, and collected, so he couldn't say he had an entire victory. "Well, that shouldn't be an issue. You will receive a dress tomorrow morning and I will send the best hairstylist to help you do your hair and makeup." Nenetl was about to speak, but Ferenc put his right index finger on his lips, giving her a shushing sound. "You will do as I say and when I say it. I will not be refused." He then unlocked the car doors, his smirk getting wider. "I look forward seeing you tomorrow."

The young woman felt a shiver go throughout her body as she opened the car door and exited. "I can't say the same thing." She closed it, walked quickly toward her house, and shut the door.

Ferenc eyed her house and chuckled. He couldn't help but feel entertained and drove off to go home. As he was driving out of the town, he still couldn't stop thinking about the previous events; his amusement slowly turned to anger. The more he thought about Boris, the more he realized that Boris had good looks and was tall. Any woman would fall for him; Nenetl looked intrigued. The realization that Nenetl seemed more interested in Boris than him made him growl in rage. Ferenc had more looks and wealth than Boris, but Nenetl wasn't interested in a poor man. He also realized his face slowly slipped, and Nenetl looked like she didn't want to be near him. It made him wonder if Nenetl would try to leave and return to Germany.

If she tried, he would not let her go.

As he drove the open road and out of the town, he noticed a young woman walking on the highway and away from the town. The way she was dressed, it looked like she was a prostitute. He knew that many women from the village would work in nearby cities, but some worked as escorts and other forms of prostitution. Many women wanted to leave the boring life of towns for opportunities. He knew that this woman was no different. He drove towards her; the woman noticed the car and was startled. The car window was opened, showing a smiling Ferenc. "Hello there, I saw you walking alone. Where are you headed?"

The young woman noticed Ferenc and blushed at him. He was handsome to her, but she couldn't help but notice his car; that was when she suspected he had money. "I'm headed to the nearby city and I was going to the bus stop."

"Would you like me to take you there? I'm heading there myself for some ...errands."

She smiled as she entered the car. Once inside, Ferenc drove off. "What's you name?"

"Csilla and yours?"

"Ferenc. If you don't mind me asking, what do you do?"

Csilla looked away as if she was embarrassed. Ferenc already knew since he knew many escorts and prostitutes. "If I had to guess, you are a sex worker."

"I-I-I-I-!"

"No need to be ashamed. You are doing everything you can to survive."

"Y-Yes. I'm trying to pay off my school; I dream of living in the city and owning a business."

Ferenc looked unamused. "Typical whores. They would instead go the easy route." That was when his urges were slowly rising, and he then drove his car to the side of the road. He took a glance at the road; no one was in sight. "So instead of working a respectable profession, you try to go the easy route and open your legs?"

Csilla noticed that Ferenc parked his car on the side of the road and slowly looked at him. He didn't look at her but noticed his emotionless eyes. "Wh-What are you talking about? You said..."

While the young woman tried to explain herself, Ferenc quietly reached down to the side of his seat and took a vaccine shot. Without warning, he stuck the shot onto Csilla's neck; she yelped. "What the hell was that!" Then, she felt her body getting weak and her mind becoming dizzy. "Wh-What did you do to me!?" Csilla tried opening the car door, but it was locked.

However, Ferenc unlocked it, letting her jump out of the car. He knew that she wouldn't get far since the drug was quickly taking effect. The businessman then reached out to another compartment with a gun and a knife. "A knife will do." Once getting the knife, he got out of his car and ensured that no one was in sight. He then walked toward the drugged woman who lost her footing and lay down on the grass.

"N-No, pleaseeeeee......" she said while slurring. The drug was entirely in effect, and Ferenc stood on top of her.

"You should consider this an honor, woman. Let's be frank: you would have never achieved your dreams. Whores never achieve the unachievable. Some may, but their luck will eventually run out when the young generation of whores come to light." He let out a sadistic smirk that would almost put the Joker's to shame. "The more of you there are, the more I will get rid of. I am angry now, but thank you for being here at the right time." He got on top of her as he tightly gripped the knife. The image of Csilla changed to the image of a woman he knew all too well. His urge got the best of him. He stabbed Csilla in the right eye. She screamed and tried to cover herself, but the drug made her body weak. Ferenc then stabbed her in the left eye; both eyeballs were on the knife.

It didn't bug him. Ferenc then undid her shirt and bra, exposing her breasts. "You wanted to use these to try to achieve your dreams. Filthy whore." He then stabbed her breasts; blood gushed out even on his clothes and face. His crazed smirk widened as he felt the blood on him; it gave him an exciting rush. He eventually stopped when he saw parts of her ribs and muscles. Ferenc breathed heavily, and he slicked his hair back. The businessman stood as he opened the trunk of his vehicle. "Consider this a favor. You would have had a useless life due to this profession." He went back and dragged the body onto the trunk and then closed it. His car had black tinted windows, so it would've made it difficult for someone to see his state.

He got out his phone and called one of his men to get the others ready to remove the body and clean his vehicle. When that was done, Ferenc drove on the road to go home. "Once I shower, I will make some calls to prepare my date for tomorrow.